The Librarian of The Haunted Library

Horror Comedy, Supernatural Suspense, Humorous Fantasy

Strangely Scary Funny

Brian Yansky

Copyright © 2023 Brian Yansky

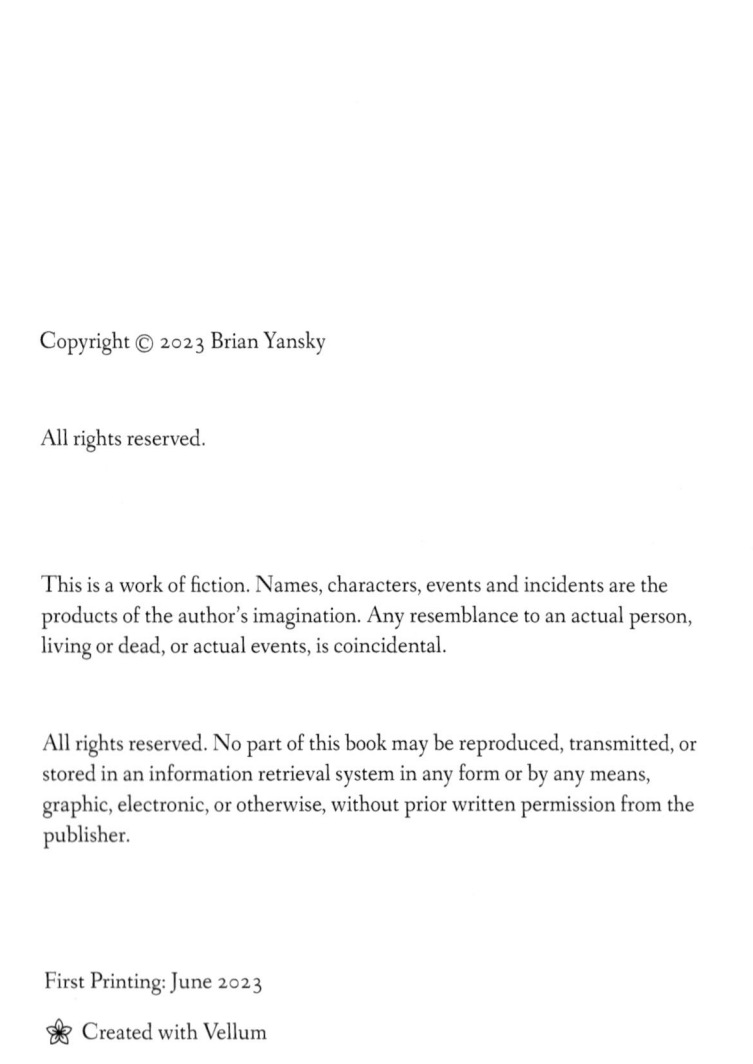

All rights reserved.

This is a work of fiction. Names, characters, events and incidents are the products of the author's imagination. Any resemblance to an actual person, living or dead, or actual events, is coincidental.

All rights reserved. No part of this book may be reproduced, transmitted, or stored in an information retrieval system in any form or by any means, graphic, electronic, or otherwise, without prior written permission from the publisher.

First Printing: June 2023

❦ Created with Vellum

Chapter One

My last foster care residence wasn't the worse place I'd lived, but I wasn't unhappy to leave the trailer, Black Widow, and Bingo. As far as foster parents went, they had the advantage of not being physically cruel, but their love of classic TV like *The Beverly Hillbillies* and *The Andy Griffith Show* bordered on psychologically abusive. It was their meth cooking in the shed that made me really nervous, though.

A few months before my eighteenth birthday, Bingo caught me calming down one of his buddies who was too high and got angry about a talking hot dog on a TV commercial. He pulled out a gun and started warning us we were all going to die if that hot dog didn't shut up immediately.

I stopped him by using suggestive hypnosis, one of my specialties. I got him to think that the hot dog was going to make him rich if he kept its secret. He left thinking he was going to be the millionaire owner of a talking hot dog.

Bingo caught on to what I'd done somehow (had a little mind reader in him maybe) and started talking to me about how we could use my gift in all kinds of ways. He threatened to mess me up if I didn't do what he told me, and then passed out. I used a dismiss hypnosis on him, taught to me by the Amazing Julie, and made him forget the entire night. He was suspicious of me after that. Even though he didn't know why, it was possible he might remember one day. I was careful around him, but every day felt like I was walking a tightrope.

When I turned eighteen, I stepped out of the trailer, took a deep breath of freedom, and walked away. I had nowhere to go, no family to turn to, and no money. The only thing I had was my ability to hypnotize people. I had always been careful with it, never using it unless I had no other choice. But now, I was alone and vulnerable. I was a little afraid of what I might have to do to survive.

I decided to go big, and used a hundred I'd stole from Bingo to take a bus to New Orleans, a city filled with mystery and magic. It was said that anything could happen there, and that was exactly what I needed, something to happen and change the direction my life was going. I boarded a bus and settled into my seat, staring out the window as the world passed by in a blur.

I arrived in New Orleans near night-fall. After a dinner of donuts and coffee in a small café that played French records, I found a grassy, shadowy area down by the river and lay out my sleeping bag. It was cold and damp even inside the bag. The nearby streets were full of noisy partiers. I couldn't sleep. When I finally nodded off, I woke almost immediately because someone had stolen my pack and was running across Jackson Square. I chased him or her. They disappeared into the thick shadows of the old city, echoes of footsteps going in all directions. I had no choice but to go back to my sleeping bag and lay awake, waiting for the thief to return. No luck.

The Librarian of The Haunted Library

I spent the next day wandering around. I kept getting lost in the maze of confusing streets. Every narrow street I walked down in the French Quarter was hugged by buildings on both sides, each building with walkways and balconies looking out over the street between. Each street had secrets, hidden courtyards, hidden pasts. The rich smells of gumbo, crawfish, jambalaya, coffee, and baking bread filled the air. They were a torture to a boy with no money.

On the positive side, New Orleans had a lot of things to see if you had a third eye (and I did)—like an old lady in a mink stole skating down Toulouse Street, her skates a few inches off the ground. She did one of those perfect turns in the air professional ice skaters do and then winked at me as she skated past. There were others. One was a ghost boy who looked like he might be from long ago. He wore a hat made of a coarse fabric, a buttoned-up shirt that was tucked into a pair of high-waisted trousers, and scuffed boots. As I approached the ghost boy, he gave me a curious smile. I thought he had been on these streets for many years, and I wondered what kept him on them. As soon as I thought this, he ran off.

I tried to sleep on a park bench; a cop in a patrolman's blue uniform with a shiny badge pinned to his front pocket woke me. He asked for identification. I did at least have my driver's license, since it had been in my pocket when my bag was stolen.

He said, "Kevin Austin?"

I told him the nuns in the orphanage gave me my birth city for a surname.

He said he could run me in for vagrancy. It was a crime to have no money. That was America for you. The cop, a nice guy, ended up giving me a few dollars and told me about a shelter. That was America for you, too.

I went to the shelter that night, but it was full.

I lay out my sleeping bag on a patch of grass down by the river on the second night. The scent of the river was cool and damp. I sat up in the dark for a long time and watched the Mississippi flow by. It was swollen fat with spring rains and the current was strong and swift. That river had been here long before humans and their cities and their other creations, and it would be here long after.

Eventually, I fell into a deep, dreamless sleep.

I woke in the morgue. The morgue was white and bright and cold and smelled of strong cleaning fluids and death. It was so quiet you could have heard a bug crawl across the floor. I was laid out naked on a metal table, a medical examiner standing over me with a scalpel. I struggled to get up, but a thick strap over my chest pinned down my arms and held me in place.

"Ah," he said. "Eyes open. That's inconvenient."

"Inconvenient?"

"Things just go more smoothly if your eyes are closed and you don't speak or move."

The man had white hair, though he was far too young for it. He was tall and thin, with deep-set eyes. He had that worn look of people who didn't sleep well.

"Undo this strap," I said. "You can see I'm not dead."

He picked up a clipboard and flipped through papers attached to it.

"I'm afraid you are according to this form. Sorry for your loss."

"I'm not," I said, hoping this was true.

"I understand how confusing this time can be," he said.

"However, the morgue only takes dead people and you are here; therefore, you are dead."

I struggled against the strap. It cut into my skin.

"What's with the straps if I'm dead?"

"You can't be too careful in this city," he said.

I did sort of get that. It was New Orleans.

"Look," I said. "I'm dead, right?"

"Afraid so."

"If I'm dead, how can I talk? Do dead people talk to you?"

"It's unusual," he said, "but you'd be surprised what goes on here. It's—"

"I know," I said. "New Orleans."

I cursed him and he said he'd give me a minute to compose myself before he started the autopsy. He left the room while I was giving him a second round of curses.

I saw the Amazing Julie sitting over on the metal table next to mine. She'd been dead for a few years. The dead I saw never spoke to me. But seeing her, a friendly familiar face, calmed me. It reminded me of what she and Master Bubba Lee always taught. You had to think when you were in trouble and you couldn't think if your mind was going in a thousand directions. Focus. Master Lee, my mentor and teacher, and The Amazing Julie, who taught me the art of hypnosis, were the two bright spots in my dark childhood.

When I looked over at the table again, Julie was gone, but I knew what I had to do. I tried my truth-teller voice. I was able to make three attempts before the medical examiner returned. Each fell short. I couldn't get the fear out of my voice. If I couldn't calm myself, it would never work.

The medical examiner leaned over me. He adjusted the light, and the glint of the scalpel blinded me for a second.

I said, "Why are you doing this?"

"There are rules," he said firmly. "Rules are rules."

I took a deep breath and spoke in a deeper hypnotic voice, each syllable like the crack of a whip. My voice echoed in the cavernous room. "Tell me why you are doing this."

His face went slack. His eyes glazed over. "I never thought when I joined the Satanist Society anything like this would be required. I just did it to pick up women. Sort of a version of Hugh Grant in that movie about the boy. You know, he pretends to have a kid. Be a single parent. But actually, he's just going to single parent meetings to meet women. That's all it was, I swear. But it seems there really is a Satan, and one of his fallen angels ordered me to do an autopsy on you, whether you were alive or dead."

"How did I get here?"

"Two other Satanists brought you in. Drugged you, I believe. And now, well, I really have no choice. I'll make it as painless as possible. You have my word."

"Why would a fallen angel want me dead? I'm nobody."

"He said you were a threat to our master and the coming of The End of Days. Really made you sound quite ominous, and here you are, just a boy. Well, it's too bad, but what can I do? An order is an order. These Satanist Societies are everywhere now. They would absolutely destroy me on social media if I let them down. You understand. No hard feelings, I hope."

I looked the medical examiner in the eye with my third eye; the one Master Lee had told me was the key to my power. I tried to hold his attention. I had to get the next voice just right, and it was harder than truth-teller. False memories could go wrong very easily.

"You remember that dream you had," I said to the medical examiner, "about your father after he died? You were marching in one of those funeral marches. Someone was playing a trombone. You remember that?"

"No," he said.

"Yes you do," I whispered. "You remember it like it was yesterday."

I managed to tap his arm once with my finger. If I could have tapped it three times, the technique that the Amazing Julie taught me would have been stronger. I was lucky, though. He wasn't resistant.

"My father is really dead?" he said, his voice breaking.

"I'm afraid so."

He started crying.

"But he whispered something to you," I said. "Do you remember that? He was in his coffin and he whispered something important."

"He did?"

"Think back. You remember? You were watching him and you heard him. His voice."

"What did he say?" he said, wiping away a tear.

"Something important," I whispered. "Something you need to hear."

"What?" he said. "What was it?"

"Undo this strap and I'll tell you."

"Please," he said. "Please tell me."

"Undo it."

He undid it.

The second he did, I hit him with a left-right combination. He wasn't a fighter, that was for sure. He was a faller. He fell to the hard, clean floor that gleamed in the bright lights. He was out cold.

"Thank you, Amazing Julie," I said. She wasn't there. It was more of a grateful acknowledgement of her and Grandmaster Bubba Lee.

I turned to the medical examiner. "When you wake, you'll know your father is alive. You will feel a sense of relief and a sense of hope for the future. You will think you need a better way to meet women. Try one of those dating apps."

I let myself out. Once outside, I breathed the city air. I had gone to sleep on a grassy patch and woke up in the morgue. Obviously, the city was sending me a message, and it wasn't subtle. Leave. As an orphan, it wasn't my first experience with being unwanted.

I walked to the highway and left the French Quarter behind. I put out my thumb. The wind whipped against my face as the cars and eighteen — wheelers whisked by. I felt alive after my brush with death. I thought of all those people going places in all those cars. An eighteen—wheeler honked its deep horn at me and the engines of all the trucks and cars roared by me. It felt good to be alive.

I didn't know where I was going and I didn't care. I was disturbed by the thought that a fallen angel had ordered my death and Satanists, apparently as well-organized as Baptists, were after me. But what could I do about it?

Move. Keep moving.

Chapter Two

A year passed: 365 days, 8760 hours, 525600 minutes.

I never settled in any place for more than a few months, often just for a few days or weeks. At first it was random, but then I started getting these messages in dreams from the cosmos. How did I know they were from the cosmos? I asked the voice in the dreams if it was from the cosmos and it said yes. The voice would give me the name of a town or city and a place to go in the town or city. I'd go there and someone would need help, and I'd help them.

It was like I was getting assignments from the universe. The voice wasn't always just in dreams. Sometimes a crow would talk to me or a person who seemed in a trance. Once it was a statue of Abraham Lincoln.

Some people might say they were from god but which one? There were thousands. I did think it was an older god, if it was a god. A new one would have texted.

It didn't really bother me not to know. The thing was, and it surprised me, I liked helping people. I'd been pretty self-focused most of my life. Also, though there were attempts on my life, there was no organized effort by the Satanists to take me out. I thought the cosmos might have something to do with that.

My very first assignment was Ms. Wang in Minneapolis. She was a small, old woman. In my dream, the voice told me she was a Supernatural. Many of the people I helped turned out to be Supernaturals.

When I first learned there were such people from Master Lee and that I was one, I felt like I was part of a very small club. But that wasn't true. Many people had talents. Most just never believed in their talents, and never used them, and the talents went back into the giant compost pile that is the universe to be used by someone who understood what they were.

Ms. Wang was a potion witch and gifted at healing, but not able to defend herself against wolves. That was why she needed me.

She was being harassed by a pack of boys who demanded weekly payments for protection from themselves. They said that when they turned into wolves, they couldn't stop themselves from devouring her and her children and grandchildren if they weren't paid.

Ms. Wang helped many people in the neighborhood, and some of those were willing to help her back. When I asked local firefighters for help, they got a long firehose from the local station and hooked it up to a fire hydrant for me. I caught up to the boys on their next visit to Ms. Wang and complimented them on their creative protection scheme. They told me to muck off.

"Do your mothers know what you're up to?" I said.

That earned me a hard look from the leader and his right-hand wolf-boy, and the others followed suit. Pack mentality. Typical among teens. It happened even when they weren't werewolves.

"She knows this is our neighborhood and we rule it," the alpha said.

"Going after a grandmother and threatening her little ones? Your mothers wouldn't mind about that?"

They all looked a little worried then. Though I'd never had a mother myself, I had noticed that most mothers, even in rougher neighborhoods, didn't like their children messing with other mothers.

"Maybe we leave this one alone?" one boy said.

"Hell we will," the alpha said. "We'll kick his ass. He won't be talking to no one."

They fanned out around me. I held up one finger.

"Just a second," I said. "Wolf rules?"

"What?" the leader said. "There ain't no wolf rules."

"Yeah, there ain't no wolf rules," the second said.

I shrugged. I looked at a boy I had standing behind me holding the firehose and he handed it to me.

"Let's show this—" the alpha said.

I interrupted him by turning on the hose and sending a blast of water their way. I knocked the leader and one other off their feet. They were screaming at me, using some very foul language. I kept the hose on them, giving them a good rinse.

"Stop it," the number two wolf boy shouted, putting up his hands in surrender.

I let the wolf boys get up, but I could see anger was getting the best of them. I didn't want any foolish aggression to ruin our blossoming friendship, so I put them down with another hard blast.

"Come on, man," one said.

The others were saying, "Come on, man, come on."

"No more collections from Ms. Wang," I said. "Leave the grandmothers alone at and the families and the people who can't afford your fees."

"That's crazy," the alpha said. "The other gangs will laugh us off the streets. We can't—"

I turned the water on. A powerful stream shot out. Several of them went down hard on the pavement. It was a teachable moment.

"All right," the alpha said, getting to his feet. "All right."

"I'm going to hold you to that," I said.

I stayed a couple of days to make sure that they kept their word. Then I moved on. I kept moving.

More years passed. More callings. Many strange things happened. It was not a bad life. It was interesting, sometimes dangerous, and it felt like I was doing something useful. That feeling of helplessness I often had as a child lost its hold over me.

Then one day I had a dream about going to a small town in East Texas named Dale where I would meet a clown. I woke up in a bad mood from that dream. I did not like clowns. They made me angry. But what could I do? I followed the dream.

Chapter Three

I met the clown at a breakfast place in Dale, Texas. It was my kind of place. A thick smell of bacon and potatoes filled the café. We were sitting on vinyl stools next to each other at a Formica counter. He had orange hair, clown paint on his face, and was wearing a polka-dot suit. There was a line of windows on the opposite wall and I could see dark clouds gathering in the sky and the wind bending small trees.

The clown had a big stack of pancakes in front of him. Some burly men sat at the tables and two scrawny meth heads sat in a booth. The only woman in the place was the waitress.

The clown smiled at me. It was a snide smile. I would have liked to punch him, but I smiled back. He asked me where I was going. My pack leaning against a stool identified me as a traveler. I told him down the road.

"I could give you a ride," he said.

I had a bad feeling. Well, sure, I always had a bad feeling around clowns, but this was more specific. This clown wasn't a Supernatural, but I could feel bad intentions radiating off him like heat from a fire.

I got in the clown's car. He tried some jokes on me that weren't funny, just racist and homophobic. It made him angry that I didn't laugh. He called me a sad sack.

He tried to get me to drink one of his beers. I was sure he'd drugged it somehow. When I refused, he reached over me to get something out of the glove compartment, but instead lifted the door handle and swung open the door. Then he kicked me out with his big clown feet. I rolled into a ditch. The clown's car sped off down the empty highway. I could hear the whine of its engine fade away as I got to my feet.

I was beat up but not hurt. I started walking down the road. It was the middle of the night and very dark. The mostly flat land became an incline. The surrounding woods thickened. After about the length of a football field, the road disappeared. Maybe for about ten steps it became a path, but after that I was just in the woods. High trees, thick leaves, the sky inky black with only the hint of stars. I stumbled over a root about the size of a redwood. I realized trying to keep going might get me in real trouble. Like break a bone or sprain an ankle trouble. Then where would I be? I didn't know where I was, but I knew I'd be in a worse place if I couldn't walk. I lay out my bag on the hill and slept at a forty-five-degree angle.

I didn't sleep badly, considering. When I woke, I was confused. The night before came back to me slowly, but when I looked around, I didn't recognize the place I was. I tried to retrace my steps, walk back to the road, but I couldn't find it. I kept walking. At first I was going downhill, but then I had to go up, and after that I realized I was getting higher and higher. The woods were just too thick and dark for me to see much, and there were no overlooks to even get a sense of where I might be, but I knew I was on a mountain.

The bright blue sky and fluffy white clouds were replaced by a heavy darkness. Everything became a dull misty gray. I shivered. It was cold but it was more than just that. Something dark and brooding moved through the woods.

I wondered, as I went up a mountain in an area of Texas where there were no mountains, how I had got so lost. This mountain couldn't be real or if it was then I couldn't be in East Texas. It was a "we're not in East Texas anymore, Toto" moment.

I kept walking because that was all I could do. I found no food or water. Days passed. Sometimes the woods were so silent all I heard was the sound of my shoes crunching through leaves and twigs. But at night I heard strange sounds. Whispers. Howling. The sound of wind but not the feel of it. The nights were long.

The screeching of monkeys woke me on the second day. The trees above me were full of them. They swung over me. I got up and ran, leaving my pack. The monkeys followed, but about a mile later, they were silent. They hadn't left, but they just sat there watching me like a jury about to convict.

Then I heard many sounds start up, as if someone had just turned on the volume. Something followed me for most of one day. I knew it was there, but I could never see it. Maybe once I saw its shadow, and it was not a lion but something like a man, only larger and with a tail. A demon? Could have been a demon.

I woke in the night, disoriented and sure something was standing over me. I pulled out my knife, but there was nothing there, nothing I could see anyway. I tried to use my third eye. More nothing.

I got up and dressed and started walking again. I heard whispering all around me. I was surrounded. I was about to be swarmed by whatever those whispers were. My heart was pounding wildly. I tried running, but I couldn't outrun them. I knew if I stopped moving, I would die. Just when I knew I couldn't go on, dawn broke and the voices faded in the light. But I knew they would be back. I knew the next night they'd overtake me.

Then, miraculously, I came to a stream rushing down from up the mountain. Just beyond I could see the roads and rooftops of a town. I collapsed on the bank of the stream. I drank long, deep gulps of water. It was so cold it hurt my throat at first. But it was sweet and cold and wet. A drink to a thirsty man is hope pushing out despair. When I'd drunk my fill, I walked into town.

Chapter Four

I'd seen many small towns in my travels. This was one of the smallest. There couldn't have been more than a couple hundred people. The square was a few red brick buildings but mostly wooden structures—houses, a few stores, a café, a bar, and a church. The roads were dirt.

A man watched me from one of the park benches in the small park at the center of the town square. He was white-haired, shaped like the traditional Santa Claus, wearing a dark suit. He waved as if we were old friends.

"Right on time," he said, looking at his wrist where a watch would be if he was wearing one. He wasn't.

"On time for what?" I asked.

"That is the question, isn't it?"

"What's the answer?"

"I don't know. But I have a feeling you're here for a reason. But is it a good reason or a bad reason? That I am not sure of."

Even though he had Santa's shape, his eyes spoiled his opportunity to let little children sit on his knee and tell him what they wanted for Christmas. They had something of the woods in them, and those woods were not for children. Unless they were the children of the dark fairy tales, abandoned and alone.

Now that I was free of the woods and in a town, I remembered them as you would a poignant nightmare—without details, but with a persistent sense of doom and despair.

"Have a hard time out there, did you, son?" he said.

"It wasn't a vacation."

He chuckled. "I like that. Yes, indeed, those woods are no vacation."

He pulled out a little notebook and wrote something in it.

"I don't see any roads out of this town," I said.

"Not today."

"Not today?"

"Is there an echo?" he said, looking around. "We do have a trail today, so that's something."

"That's good," I said, uncertainly.

"They aren't trustworthy," he said. "Like to trick people. Take them places they don't want to go. Quicksand. Off cliffs. That sort of thing. Watch yourself should you go back into the woods."

"That sounds like the opposite of what trails are supposed to do in my experience," I pointed out.

"No trail has a chance against Mother Nature. Truth is, one day all our trails will be gone and we'll be gone and Mother Nature will still be here."

"Where am I?" I asked.

"Eden," he said.

His bench was just to the right of a large tree, and I couldn't help looking up for a giant snake curling its way down the tree's branches. When it spoke, I knew what it

The Librarian of The Haunted Library

would sound like. It would have the soothing, slithering voice of Karl.

"Sit down here, young man. I'd like to give you some advice."

I sat on the bench beside him. The sun was going down. I hated to see that. I wasn't ready for another long night.

"I think I'm feeling a little light-headed," I said.

"It's the altitude. Takes some getting used to."

"I haven't eaten in three days."

"I'm mayor of this town. I have decided to welcome you to Eden. You will not be run off. You remind me of Sir Francis Drake, second man to navigate the globe, pirate, and adventurer. A bit of a scamp, but he kept things interesting."

He sounded like he'd known the man personally.

"Kevin," I said, sticking out my hand.

"You look weary, Kevin."

"I am."

"How'd you find yourself in our haunted woods?"

He pulled out his notebook again.

"A clown pushed me out of a car," I said.

"What state were you in?"

"I don't know. Upset."

"State," he said. "Which of the fifty?"

"The piney woods of Texas," I said.

He wrote my answer in his little notebook.

"Welcome to Eden. You look around, then go over to Lucy's café and tell her the mayor said to put your dinner on the mayor's tab."

"Thanks," I said.

"If someone invites you into their house, you might want to decline until you get to know which ones are safe."

"OK," I said, but it wasn't.

"Do you believe in reincarnation?" he asked.

"I don't disbelieve in it."

"Good answer," he said. "My office is over there where it says Mayor's Office. Come and see me tomorrow. Feel free to sleep in the park tonight. Safer than the woods."

Which wasn't saying much.

"Thank you," I said.

"Some of us believe we are dead, and this is the place we come to have our souls weighed and our future determined. Yours is an old soul. If we are correct, you would do wise to reflect on your life. Perhaps you'll get another."

If he was right, I'd been killed by a clown. Talk about a disappointing death. I didn't believe I was dead, but I was pretty sure this town wasn't one you could find on a map. So where was I?

Chapter Five

I walked around Eden. It took me under ten minutes to see everything. The church was the most imposing building on the square. It was made of brick and had stained glass windows and a bell tower. There was a sign on the front black oak doors that said OUT OF ORDER. Then I realized it actually read The Church of Out of Order.

I wasn't sure what that meant, but I sort of liked the sound of it.

The main street went on past the square, but only for a few blocks. There were houses along it. There was something beyond the houses, a little farm maybe. Then beyond that, in a clearing, a large white stone house. There were four narrow streets off the main street, crooked and thin like the legs of an insect. The town had the shape of a Charlie Brown Christmas tree.

At the end of one of those streets, a little off into the gnarly trees, was a large old house with colored glass windows and four chimneys on a crooked roof. It wasn't just the roof that was crooked, though. The entire house seemed like a person of advanced years trying to get out of an armchair after one too many whiskeys. It sagged in places and jutted out in others. A sign out on the front yard read Eden Library. It looked more like a haunted house. As soon as I had the thought, I heard a rattling of chains.

I went back down the uneven and now slightly wobbly street. Maybe I was wobbly. It was hard to tell.

There were no vehicles anywhere in the town. There was a donkey in one of the front yards. She wore a straw hat. Her lips peeled back, and she grinned at me. I couldn't tell if she was being friendly or threatening. There was a graveyard just west of town. There were several fresh graves which, in a town of that size, were disturbing.

My last stop was Lucy's café. I planned to order one of everything off the menu. Really. Not really. Really. Then tomorrow, after sleeping in the square, I'd see the mayor and, I hoped, he would tell me how to get out of Eden and the woods with a single day's travel. I knew this was unlikely, but I needed to think it was possible. The thought of another night in the woods gave me a chill.

I opened the door and went into the cafe. It was small, with half a dozen red vinyl booths over by the windows and about as many Formica table tops in the center of the room. There were a dozen round cushioned stools lined up at the counter. A chocolate cake under a plastic lid was on display at the far end.

There were what appeared to be two couples in one of the window booths and three old ladies in another; two singles at the tables, and no one at the counter. Conversation stopped when I walked in and the townspeople looked me over. By the time I sat at the counter, people were talking again.

Outside, the sun had slipped out of sight. The air was

turning. Darkness seemed to cover the town almost immediately. It was almost like something monstrous cast a shadow. In that second, before it was completely dark, I saw a woman with a striking figure and no head. She seemed to be carrying something. I couldn't see what, but I could make a guess.

"Just you?" the waitress said, holding a menu. She was about my age, black hair, brown eyes, pretty.

She handed me a menu.

"Just me," I said. "The mayor said to put my dinner on his tab."

"Did he? You're new around here. I never forget a face."

"How many faces are there in this town?"

"Varies. Last count, 188. How long were you lost?"

"I'm still lost," I said.

"Don't be coy. It's beneath you."

"How do you know?"

"The question remains."

"Three nights," I said.

"You look like a hiker."

"Hitch-hiker," I said.

"How exotic."

I told her about the clown.

"That's terrible," she said.

"It is," I admitted. "Beaten up by a clown. Do many people get lost in the woods and stumble into Eden?"

"Everybody in this town got here the same way, except for the four teenagers found as babies on the steps of the church."

"That's very strange," I said.

She shrugged. "Some people spent weeks in the haunted woods. They were nearly insane by the time they found Eden. Most are like you, three or four days."

"But some people must have been born here."

"Why?"

"Why what?"

"Must some people have been born here?"

She had a point.

"No one knows how they got here?" I said. "They just wandered into the piney woods and they're here?"

"I don't know what the piney woods are, but yes."

"Here," I said, "Wherever here is."

"Exactly," she said.

"Um," I said. "I thought I just saw a woman carrying her head a few minutes ago. You wouldn't know anything about that, would you?"

"Lady Blackstone," she said.

"Oh," I said. "Lady Blackstone. Right."

"From England. She and her husband. Lord Blackstone. He was thirty-third in line for the crown. I think those thirty-two before him are lucky he got lost and ended up here in Eden."

"The lady carries her head," I said.

"What else would she do with it?"

"I'm finding this all a little strange."

"Just a little?"

"Good point."

The order up bell dinged. She told me she'd be back after she delivered the Sanchez's their food.

I stared blankly at the menu. I was having trouble deciding.

"What can I get for you?" the waitress said when she got back to me a few minutes later. She held her pad up and flicked the ball-point pen in her other hand.

"How do people get off the mountain down to a town or down to anywhere?" I asked.

"But here?"

"I didn't say that," I said.

"Implied," she said.

"People must go into town."

"Maybe," she said. "Sometimes people leave, but they never come back if they do. Many think the reason they don't come back is that they can't."

"Once off the mountain, you're off the mountain?"

"Seen the tower off in the woods?"

"Yes."

"Lord Blackstone's tower. He's said before he's seen a few wander away from Eden and down the mountain, but he's never seen one make it all the way down. Most think they don't come back because they're dead."

"That's disappointing," I said.

"Yes," she said.

"The mayor thinks we're already dead."

"He's a deadhead."

"A what?" I said.

"That's what they call themselves. The folks who think we're already dead. They have a little group. Meets here on Wednesday nights usually. Personally, I'd be put out if this is the afterlife."

"None I've heard of seem all that great," I said. "Heaven, boring. Hell, well, obviously terrible. Valhalla, day after day of fighting and partying, sounds good at first, but it must get to be too much, eventually. Hades and Tartarus both seem pretty bleak. Worse weather than Fargo or Buffalo."

"We aren't dead," she said. "Have you decided what you want?"

"Reincarnation seems a little pointless if you can't

remember anything. Over and over. Not necessarily getting better or worse."

"Enough with the afterlife," she said. "How about some dinner?"

I told her I wanted breakfast if they made breakfast for dinner and she said they did and that she usually ate breakfast for dinner herself.

"Sometimes I even eat dinner for breakfast," she said. "Not that often, though."

"If we were really dead," I said, "we wouldn't have to eat, would we?"

She shrugged.

I ordered pancakes and bacon and sausage and scrambled eggs and French Toast and coffee and orange juice and milk.

"Got it," she said. "The mayor didn't realize what he was letting himself in for."

"I'm pretty hungry."

"I'm Olive," the waitress said.

"I'm pretty hungry is not my name," I said.

"Could have fooled me," she said.

We smiled at each other. We were trying to show each other we were friendly. Humans did that. I was pretty sure she was human. I wasn't so sure about the lady carrying her own head around.

"You look like someone who might be good at helping people with a problem," Olive said.

"You have a problem?" I said.

She hesitated, seemed almost ready to tell me something, but then we were interrupted.

A man started choking. He was handsome, somewhere in his thirties, dressed in a suit. I hadn't really noticed him beyond that, but I saw now that he had something, a kind of

The Librarian of The Haunted Library

movie-star quality, even as his face turned red and he dropped to the floor. I thought someone would administer the Heimlich maneuver, but no one moved. I glanced over at the window and thought I saw shadows out there. No one rushed in, though. I got down on my knees and into a sitting position and pulled him back toward me and worked a fist under his solar plexus.

"Google Heimlich Maneuver," I shouted at Olive.

"No google up here," she said. "No internet."

I thought everyone had internet. I'd seen pictures of Buddhist monks in a Tibetan monastery on a mountain so high clouds floated out their window texting.

I tried to apply the pressure in little upward thrusts, but nothing came out of his mouth. I laid him down to do CPR, but he was foaming at the mouth, something yellow and a lot of it. I tried to wipe it away but more just came out. He had a dead person's eyes. I saw his spirit float out of the body with my third eye. He was trying to grab at me, fighting to stay, but a second later, he was pulled up out into the night.

Olive went over to a red phone on the counter. It had a cord. She punched buttons on it. I could hear her tell someone that the librarian was dead.

"Oatmeal," Olive said into the phone. Pause. Then. "I know. How do you choke on oatmeal?"

"He's gone," I said. "I'm sorry."

Olive said he had been the librarian. That was a surprise. He didn't look like a librarian. I'd have gone with hit-man or mafia boss.

She said she was calling Doc. Three minutes later, Doc and Lucy arrived. Lucy was a tall woman. Blonde. Older, maybe fifties, attractive. The doctor was a small white-haired man with artistic fingers.

"Oatmeal?" Lucy said to Olive, and they both shook their heads.

The Doc looked him over. "I don't think he choked to death. Poisoned."

I thought this was a Sherlock Holmes level deduction, but it turned out so many librarians had been poisoned, most anyone in Eden would have made the same guess.

Lucy said, "We're very careful not to poison our oatmeal."

"I'll take care of him," Doc said.

"Excuse me, Doc," I said. "But isn't it a little late for that?"

"Doc is also the Undertaker," Olive said.

Seemed like a conflict of interest to me, but I said nothing.

Over a dozen townspeople were gathered in the café by then, including the mayor, who told me he was also the constable. Doc asked two young men to carry the librarian down to his office.

Olive told the mayor-constable about how I'd tried to save the librarian.

"A man of action," the mayor said. "I had a feeling about you."

"Except," I felt the need to point out. "He's dead."

"You did the best you could," an old woman who looked a lot like Mother Teresa said, "but the Librarian has read his last book."

"He was a man, take him for all in all, I shall not look upon his like again," another woman said. "And I wouldn't want to."

"Don't be too sure," another old woman said.

There was some discussion on this point. Some believed in reincarnation and others brought up zombies, both

The Librarian of The Haunted Library

exceptions to the claim you wouldn't look on the dead again.

"Anyway, that's not what I meant. You know what he was."

"I don't want to speak ill of the dead," another woman said.

"Then don't," Lucy said. "This isn't the time or place."

"A man like that," another woman said. "You live by the sword; you die by the sword. Who said that?"

"If by sword you mean—"

The mayor interrupted the women. "He wasn't the best or the worst librarian we've had."

Many in the crowd seemed to agree. I thought it was pretty tepid approval. Not what you'd want on your tombstone regardless of what your occupation was—*He wasn't the best or worst doctor. He wasn't the best or worse exterminator.* It wasn't even good enough to put in a commercial.

"Long live the new librarian," a very small man said. He couldn't have been five feet tall.

In fact, he was small enough that I would call him a little person. He had a large head. I noticed a woman stood next to him, the same height but beautiful. She had thick, long blonde hair. It may have been the most beautiful hair I'd ever seen.

The little man was looking at me and so was the little woman and they both said, "Long live the Librarian" again and I began to notice how everyone was looking at me now.

I noticed something on the floor. It glittered. Like sun on a shard of glass. I bent over and picked it up. It was a gold ring with a black stone at the center and an L carved into the stone.

"Was this his?" I said.

I held it up.

"Try it on," the mayor said.

"What?" I said.

"Go on," he said. "See if it fits."

"Mayor," Olive said, disapprovingly. "Mayor, don't."

"Yes, do," the little woman and the little man said together. "Try it on, young man."

The little woman's voice was so calm and comforting, almost like a mother's voice, and I had never had a mother. I had the urge to want to make the little woman happy, maybe even to make her proud. It made no sense, but the feeling got stronger. I put the ring on.

It fit. I held it up. "Look at that."

"Take it off," Olive said. "You don't want the job. You don't know what you're getting into."

"Long live the new librarian," the mayor said, "though as we all know, it is likely more a hope than a prediction."

The people in the café clapped.

"I don't understand," I said. Also, the words *hope than a prediction* had sort of stuck in my mind like a thorn in the hand.

"The job is yours," the mayor said.

"What job?" I said.

I tried to take off the ring. It was stuck. It had slipped right on, but it wouldn't even move up to the knuckle. My finger had swollen, or the ring had shrunk.

"Librarian, of course."

I looked at Olive. She shook her head, sort of like you would at a child who had done something foolish.

"Is this a joke?" I said.

"There's a dead man lying on the floor," the mayor said.

"No time for joking," the little man said.

The crowd made a noise of agreement.

The Librarian of The Haunted Library

"But I don't have the education or experience to be a librarian," I said in my most reasonable voice.

"You have the ring," the mayor said. "It fits."

I tried again to get it off my finger. No movement.

"Room and board," the mayor said. "The town will pay for you to have one meal a day at Lucy's and provide you with groceries and a small salary. What do you say?"

"I'm not a librarian," I said. "I'm a traveler. And I will be moving on. It's what I do."

"Not really an occupation," the little man said.

Several in the crowd repeated what he'd said. "Not really an occupation." "No, no, not an occupation." Others made agreeing sounds.

"You like books?" the mayor asked.

"I love books. I read all the time. If I'm really into a novel, the only way you can get it is to pry it from my cold, dead hands."

"Why would I do that?"

I looked around, and everyone looked uneasy.

"You've heard that before," I said. "The gun nuts? They say it."

"No one kills someone over a book, though," the mayor said.

"No, they say it about guns. I was just being ironic or something."

"I think you mean satirical," the little woman said.

"I think you're right," Olive said.

I bet someone had killed someone over a book. People had killed other people for just about every reason you could imagine. I didn't say this.

"You can handle yourself in a fight. Seen ghosts. Wolves that become men. Fought a witch. Talked to a god. Walked through haunted woods." The mayor wasn't asking questions. He knew things about me somehow. It bothered me that he knew them.

"I never went to college, so I can't really be a librarian," I said.

"College, smallage," the little man said.

"The job is yours," the mayor said.

"Maybe you should think it over," Olive said. She mouthed the word refuse.

The rest of the crowd encouraged me to take the job.

"You'll love it here," the little woman said.

"Love it," the little man said.

A big crow flew up to the picture window of the café. Its wings flapped noisily as it flew in place. It cawed. It bumped up against the glass. Everyone looked uneasy. That bird seemed deranged. Maybe it had rabies. Could birds even get rabies?

"Will you be our new librarian?" the mayor said. His voice boomed over the bird's caws, flapping wings, and bumps against the window.

"You have to understand. I'm a traveler. I'm happy to be here now, but soon I'll have to leave."

"Fine," the mayor said. "You can leave any time you want. Will you take the job?"

"I can leave any time?" I said. "I'd give you a few days' notice, of course. But I will be moving on like I always do."

"Understood. Your answer, please?"

I probably should have thought over the offer more. One important point that I didn't consider fully was that the former librarian had been poisoned. Of course, it was unlikely that the job itself (being a librarian wasn't considered a particularly dangerous occupation) had anything to do with his being poisoned. Still. I should not have rushed into accepting the position.

The Librarian of The Haunted Library

I needed the money, though. Also, who else in all the world was going to offer me a job as a librarian?

"All right," I said, and I shook the mayor's hand. "I'll take the job."

The bird stopped cawing and flew off.

"With the hand that has the ring on it, please," the mayor said.

I shook his hand with my left.

"It is official," the mayor said. "We have a new librarian."

The crowd clapped.

The door opened and a cold wind blew in. The room got very quiet. The crowd parted as a man walked through it. He had long, black hair and wore a black suit with a long coat seriously out of fashion, like a couple of hundred years. He had excessively blue eyes, and a pronounced sneer. A thin man, his fingers were long and artistic, like a piano player strangler.

"No," he said to the mayor. "Stop this now."

He was a man, but he had the glow of magic over him. I could see with my third eye he was a magician.

"The librarian died, Lord Blackstone," the mayor said. "You weren't here. This young man was. The library chose him."

"You chose him," Lord Blackstone said.

"The young man has the ring."

"You promised the job to me."

"You know I couldn't do that. I was rooting for you, but the library chooses."

"I was on my way."

"You were detained, weren't you?" the mayor said in a way that sounded a lot to me like *checkmate*. "If you were the one, you would have been here."

The two men locked eyes. They were both tall, but Lord Blackstone was thin and had the loose look of someone snake-like fast with a strike. The mayor was bell-shaped but sturdy and had Lord Blackstone by at least fifty, sixty pounds.

"Give me the ring," Lord Blackstone said to me.

"I'm having trouble getting it off," I said. "Maybe some soap."

"Another sign he is the right choice," the mayor said. "The ring fits. It isn't coming off without someone cutting off his finger."

"Let's not be too hasty," I said.

"That can be arranged," Lord Blackstone said.

"You're too late," the mayor said.

The crowd was waiting for something to happen. Maybe for Lord Blackstone to punch me or turn me into a duck. I don't think they wanted it to happen, necessarily, but they certainly didn't want to miss it if it did. That was human. News stations knew all about this. People couldn't help themselves from watching terrible things. If someone tried to have a station of all good news, they'd probably have about two people watching. But I bet those two people would feel a lot better after twenty minutes of good news than the rest of us after watching the other news.

"Who are you?" Lord Blackstone said, looking at me. He was really looking, which was disconcerting.

"Kevin," I said.

"No," he said. "You're someone. Were you at last year's National Dark Arts Convention?"

"Were you?" I said.

"Of course not. But I watched it on TV. We do get TV up here."

"I wasn't there," I said.

The Librarian of The Haunted Library

"'This is our Dark Arts expert, Lord Blackstone," the mayor said.

"Who is Kevin?" Lord Blackstone said asked the mayor.

"I am," I answered.

"He is the librarian," the mayor said.

"I'm just passing through," I said.

"You hear that?" Lord Blackstone said to the room. "He's passing through. And you all conspired to give away my job to him. You stood against me. I won't forget."

"We told the mayor the job was yours," the little man said. "But what's done is done."

"Kevin," Lord Blackstone said. "Where have I heard that name before? Hand over the ring, Kevin, and I won't turn you into smoke."

"Can you really do that?" I asked.

The little man piped in before Lord Blackstone could answer. "Saw him do it to that plumber fella when he handed him the bill."

"Plumbing work is always expensive," the mayor said.

"This was excessive," Lord Blackstone said.

"Anyway, you're too late, Lord Blackstone," the mayor said. "He has the ring. Nothing anyone can do."

Lord Blackstone gave me an especially nasty look. It was a good one. I didn't fault the look. It was just that I'd seen it before.

"Is this about library fines, Lord Blackstone?" I said, trying diversion hypnosis.

"What?" he said. "What are you talking about?"

"For my first act as librarian, I'm making this next week amnesty week to everyone who has a fine."

"I knew you would be a good one," the little woman said. "I have a book that's a year overdue. Still count?"

"Of course," I said.

"Stop this," Lord Blackstone said.

"Stop what?"

"Whatever it is you're doing."

"I'm offering amnesty. To you. To everyone. Return your library materials. No fines. My treat."

"I don't have any books."

"Something on magic, I'm guessing."

He looked a little guilty.

"Give me the ring and I may let you walk out of Eden unharmed," he said.

I couldn't help noticing the word *may*.

Part of me wanted to give him the ring and walk out of town, but I didn't like being told what to do. Also, I couldn't get it off.

He didn't have much in the way of lips but what he had pressed against each other furiously. His eyes narrowed. I thought he was about to raise a wand and strike me with a bolt of lightning.

"You'll regret it," he predicted and stormed out the door.

"He really doesn't want to return that book," I said.

"You are a bit of a character, aren't you?" the mayor said.

"A fool," Olive said, but she smiled when she said it.

Chapter Six

"I think it's time we get you to your new home, librarian," the mayor said, slapping me on the back.

"Thank you, mayor," I said.

"I'm the constable now. Escorting the new librarian is the constable's job."

This was going to be confusing. The constable and the mayor looked too much alike.

"You'd better take this," Olive said, handing me a sandwich as I walked toward the door.

"Thanks," I said. "I guess I'll be seeing you."

She looked a little sad when she handed me the sandwich. I was a little sad because I didn't get pancakes and eggs and bacon and sausage and French toast.

We went out the door. The bells jingled. The crowd watched us walk away. We went across the square through the little park. The mayor kept nervously looking back. I was looking up. I hadn't seen the night sky for three nights. Stars and a full moon. They were reassuring.

"Lord Blackstone is a powerful magician?"

"Couldn't be president of our chapter of the Dark Arts Society if he wasn't."

"Lot of evil people in Eden?" I asked. Some things are good to know when you're a stranger. I'd been a stranger everywhere I went since leaving Texas almost seven years ago. Before, too, if I'm honest. Stranger in new foster homes, new kid in two different orphanages. I'd got used to coming into a place where not everyone welcomed me.

"Maybe no more than other small towns, but the quality of evil is higher. Not a lot of amateurs."

"I appreciate a job well done," I said.

"Still," he said. "There is more good than bad here."

"But not much more," I said.

"It is always a close race."

The library was lit up by a full moon. It looked like it had shifted, leaning more to the left than in the afternoon. The colors of the windows were in different places. It looked like a haunted house. In this case, a haunted library.

"How do you have electricity up here?" I asked the mayor.

"We have our own generator."

We went up the stairs to the wraparound porch.

"Press your ring into the lock on the door," the mayor said.

I saw the indentation in the wood in the shape of an L just above the doorknob. I pressed the ring into it. The door opened; a loud yawning creak went on for a few seconds. Lamps at tables and in corners lit up. A quick glance at the living room and the kitchen was enough for me to make an educated guess that every room was filled with books. What had once been a kitchen was now a special collection of mysteries. Looking at the titles, I saw that the word mystery was used more broadly than a genre of fiction.

One thing was that it was much larger inside than outside. It was defying some natural laws but this town seemed to be pretty good at that.

"Great place for a bookish ghost to haunt," I said.

"The ghost is most certainly bookish."

"A name I would recognize?"

"All I know is he was a writer before he became the librarian. Died when he was attacked by a polar bear."

"What was a polar bear doing here?"

"What are any of us doing here?" he said.

Good point.

"Is the library open to the townspeople?" I asked.

"For two hours a day, 9-11, and by appointment."

"Can they borrow books?"

"Certainly. If the book agrees."

"If the book agrees?"

"It will let you know if it doesn't."

"The book will tell me?"

"Naturally. *Heart of Darkness* is a bit testy. In fact, it may wake you from time to time yelling *The horror, The horror*. Don't be alarmed."

What had I got myself into?

We walked into the living room. It was a pleasant room, with all the bookcases completely filled. The only spaces on the walls not devoted to books were windows. The furniture was a little nicer than you'd expect—more 19th century gentleman's library than public one—sofa, two armchairs, lamps on tables, a few other reading chairs around the room, each with reading lamps of one kind or another by them. It all looked like it was from a few centuries ago but in pristine condition.

There was a stairway to the second floor. The stained wood banister had a railing with a snake's head on the end.

Python was my guess. In the way I saw some things, I saw that the railing had once been alive and had been turned to wood by a magician or witch.

I went over and put my hand on the railing. It felt like a snake's skin and then like wood. The mayor didn't follow me. He stayed near the front door.

"It's a house full of books," he said.

"That it is," I agreed.

"Are you, perchance, a religious man?" The mayor asked. "Have any special gods you pray to?"

"I don't."

"Might be good to find one. You could use the help."

"Who would you recommend?"

"I pray to the Mountain."

"I suppose he or she is easiest to reach," I said.

"Exactly. I think proximity is important in a god. It's a she."

"Have a name?"

"Clementine," he said. "Rumor is she's a self-made god. Started off a mortal. Grew up on a pig farm."

"Down to earth?" I said.

"For a god," he said.

"Maybe I'll try her."

I liked the idea of self-made god. A god of the people, from the people. Not many of those around.

"You think Lord Blackstone poisoned the librarian?" I asked.

"Former librarian," he reminded me. "It's possible."

"Who else might have poisoned him?"

"Exactly. You'll do just fine at this job if you keep asking the difficult questions. I have confidence you'll find who killed your predecessor."

"I'll find who killed him?"

"Exactly what I just said."

"Aren't you the constable?"

"The librarian takes care of murders. All serious crimes and acts of evil fall under the librarian's jurisdiction. Look at the job description. Did you not know that?"

"You know I didn't."

"Don't blame me," he said. "You took the job. I simply offered it to you."

Lawmen upheld the law. Librarians took care of books. They took care of libraries. They helped people find information. They collected for their collections. They didn't find murderers and solve crimes.

"I think you might have a limited idea of what a librarian is," he said.

"Apparently so," I said. "I do take care of the books, though, right?"

"They don't require a lot of care. Very self-sufficient books. Unless, of course, someone or something escapes from one of them."

I wasn't even going to ask. I was very tired and still hungry. I wanted to eat my sandwich and collapse into bed.

"And the collection downstairs," he said. "Some things in that are quite rare."

"More books?"

"Not exactly. Let's just stick to the upstairs for now, though. More details later."

"Should we go look upstairs?" I said.

"Only the librarian goes upstairs or down to the basement. If someone wants a book from the second floor, you go get it for them. If the book agrees, you bring it down. The second floor is, well, versatile."

"What does that mean?"

"Just be firm if they disobey. They need to know who is

the boss. Also, it changes from day to day. That part of the house likes variety."

I was trying to process what he was telling me. It wasn't going well.

"Your apartment is downstairs in the basement. It's quite nice. Also, as I mentioned, the other collection is downstairs."

"Collection of what, though?"

"The librarians call it the Collection of Curiosities. That should give you some idea."

"Dangerous?"

"Most definitely."

"Evil or good?"

"A little good and a little bad is my understanding.".

"You know that I have no idea what I'm doing here. I'm not a magician. If Lord Blackstone turns me into a mouse, I won't be able to turn myself back into myself. Can you turn me back?"

"Probably not," he said. "But Lord Blackstone is more likely to turn you into a cloud of dust if he decides to turn you into anything. He wouldn't chance your survival."

"Comforting."

He shrugged. Even though I couldn't read shrugs, I got the meaning of this one. It wasn't his concern.

"The former librarian wasn't the first librarian to be murdered, was he? Even though I'm pretty sure he had special abilities."

"Magician, first class. Even Lord Blackstone was careful around him."

"Not the first to be murdered?"

The mayor looked at where a watch would be on his wrist if he wore a watch, which he didn't. "Goodness now.

The Librarian of The Haunted Library

Look at the time. I'm afraid I'm late. See you tomorrow, librarian."

He gave a little wave as he left the library. Fast for a man his size. I would have had to run to catch him.

"I know you don't have a watch," I shouted as he ran out the door.

I went down the stairs. I looked for a light switch and didn't see one. Lights from above, soft lights, came on as I passed and I could see my way. The lights followed me down the stairs and then down the hall. Behind me, the lights died and darkness returned.

The door to the apartment (I hoped) had a place for the ring. I put my ring into it and the door swung open. The apartment was nice. The living room had old furniture and a built-in bookcase, a TV, and an adequate kitchen. There was a bathroom with a big bathtub and two bedrooms, one large and one small, both with queen-size beds. I liked both rooms. I would sleep in both.

The apartment was all there was to the basement. If there was a second library in the basement (as the mayor had said) then it must be hidden or there was another stairway down from another part of the library.

The fridge had food in it and Eden beer. The label had a picture of Adam and Eve sharing one of the Eden beers. I drank one while I ate my sandwich. Not bad.

What was I going to do?

For starters, I was going to sleep in the smaller room.

I lay down in a very soft bed. I heard a common ghost *Whooo-ooo-oooooooo-oo* and some chain rattling from upstairs. It was comforting. If the library had a ghost, then I must not be dead. You couldn't have someone dead haunting you if you were dead. It wouldn't make sense. A ghost's best card was that they were dead, from the great beyond none of us knew about, and they had come back. And they were out to do us wrong. Maybe even drag us into death with them. But If I was dead already, where was the threat?

Therefore, I must be alive. That was a relief. Now, if I could just stay that way.

Eventually, I got to sleep.

I had some troubling dreams.

In one, I woke up as a cockroach, which I knew would really bother my wife. She hated bugs. I was grossed out a little and also confused. When did I get a wife?

Another nightmare was a true event. A foster mother who burned me with lit cigarettes to make a cross on my back. She had decided that I was possessed by a demon named Billy. He was a woke demon she said who approved of all kinds of terrible evils like homosexuality and green cards for immigrants trying to destroy America with their foreign ways. She would punish him and me.

After I'd been taken away from her and sent to another home, she murdered one of the babies she was supposed to take care of because she said the baby was talking in tongues backwards, a sure sign of the devil.

The foster care system I was in did something similar to what the Catholic church did with priests who were molesting young boys; the church moved the priests to another parish when they caught them and so spread a plague of molestations; the foster-care system moved a kid when a foster parent did something like the one who burned me. They gave them new children to foster until they did something they couldn't hide, like the woman who killed the baby.

They did this for years and years.

I read this book by Kurt Vonnegut about half a dozen

times called *Slaughter House Five*. In the novel, when humans do terrible things, sad and evil and disappointing things, the narrator often says, *So it goes*. There's a deep sadness in the phrase and also a hopelessness.

I went back to sleep after these two nightmares and then I had the worst nightmare of all. I was in a bar down in a basement. It was smokey. I was sitting at the bar on a barstool drinking a glass of whiskey. I was the only one there. He sat down on a bar stool next to mine.

"Karl," he said.

"I know who you are," I said.

"Good. It's time. I need you."

"Need me for what?"

"You know what. Chance of a lifetime. Eternal life. Wealth beyond your imagination. Fame. Anything you want. Women love powerful, evil men. You'll work for me. Public relations. Give up this sham of helping people. Fulfill the prophecy."

I heard a flutter of wings.

He swore. "They can't keep you from me forever."

I woke. My bed was wet with sweat. I was breathing like I'd just run a sprint. The room must have been a hundred degrees. I'd had this dream several times. Three times, maybe four. It kept coming back. It haunted me.

I got up and went over to the bookcase. I pulled out *Oliver Twist* and took it back to bed. I fell asleep after an hour or two. No more nightmares.

Chapter Seven

I woke up to the smell of bacon, which was pretty frickin awesome until I remembered it was also impossible. I wondered out to the kitchen, and I saw someone in the kitchen cooking. That was a surprise. She had her back to me, but I could see she was older by her shape and the gray hair up in a neat bun. I knew that bun and the way she stood, sturdy as a linebacker.

"Hello," I said. "Excuse me."

I looked around for a weapon. Pots hung from hooks over the stove, but she was between me and them. The knives were in a wooden block on the other side of the kitchen. I was just going to have to take her with my hands. I should be able to take a senior citizen who wore her hair in a bun. She wouldn't be the first little old lady I'd faced though generally, at some point, they showed their true selves, something monstrous and deadly. But I'd never faced this particular old lady. This one who was one of the few foster-care bright spots from my childhood.

She looked over her shoulder at me; it was her all right. Mrs. Johnson, who happened to be dead, and the only foster mother who had really cared for me enough, she wanted to adopt me. She would have too if she hadn't had a heart-attack the day she made her decision.

She had a spatula in her hand and was flipping bacon. Scrambled eggs and toast were already on a plate.

"Mrs. Johnson?" I said.

"Come and sit down, Kevin. It's almost ready."

I sat at the table. I picked up the fork from the setting. Some people would have chosen a spoon or butter knife, but I'd take a fork every time. Gouge an eye out. Stab a heart if it came to it. I hoped it didn't. There was the tiniest chance it was her, but if it was, she must be dead and if she was dead, I doubt a stab wound with a fork or spoon or butter knife was going to make much difference.

Smokey smell of bacon filled the room. She used tongs to move it from a skillet to the plate.

"Can I help you?" I said.

"You just sit right there and let me do this for you."

It had been a long time since someone who didn't work in a restaurant had made me breakfast. She came over with the plate and set it in front of me. I had the fork ready for a fight or food. She backed away to the counter.

"You aren't eating?" I asked.

"Oh, I don't eat, dear," she said.

I couldn't resist. If it was poisoned, I was a goner because I ate with abandon. Sometimes you just had to. Tasted great.

"The dead don't eat?" I asked, my mouth full.

"Don't talk with your mouth full," she said.

"Sorry," I said, taking a big bite of bacon.

Nothing like being lost in haunted woods to work up an appetite.

"You must be about twenty-eight by now?" she said.

"That's right," I said.

"And you've never settled down?"

"Harder to hit a moving target," I said.

She frowned. She didn't approve of self-pity. So that was just like Mrs. Johnson. That frown. She leaned back against the counter and folded her arms in front of her.

"No woman in your life?"

Something was off. Then I realized what it was.

"You forgot the glasses," I said. She always wore these small granny glasses.

"Let's say I took them off to cook," she said.

"How's Mr. Johnson?"

"I can make you some more," she said. "I can make you anything you want."

"He was the cook of the family. I guess you've had time to learn things since you died."

"You always were a good eater," she said.

"I appreciate your saying that," I said.

I did because I really wasn't a good eater back then, and it just helped confirm what I knew pretty much from the moment I saw her. Here was a monster in disguise. I'd better be ready.

"I forgot your coffee," she said, pouring me a cup and bringing it over.

She sat it down. When I reached for it, she took a stab at my heart with a knife she had in her left hand. I rocked the chair away from it. Then I threw hot coffee into her face. She hissed and backed away. The chair tipped over and I landed on the floor. I'd lost my fork.

"This is unacceptable behavior," she said.

Her fingers became claws, long curved black ones. She walked over to me quick-step and swiped at me. I rolled to my feet, coffee cup in my hand, and used the cup to block some power. Then the cheek I'd hit with the ring began to sizzle. She staggered back, grabbing her face. It was burning.

I slid around her and grabbed the largest knife in the knife box on the counter. I stabbed her in the heart. It didn't have the effect I expected, so I stabbed her six quick stabs before she could put out the fire that had burned half her face.

She managed to knock me back against the wall before I got in a seventh stab. She'd lost half her face by then, though. She retreated and disappeared. The breakfast disappeared with her.

I felt cheated. I was hungry. Imaginary food was not very filling.

I took a shower to ease the pain and stiffness and wash off the blood. The hot water felt good. When I got out, I toweled off and dressed.

Not the best start to my first day on the job.

As I went up the stairs, I heard rattling chains.

I was pretty sure the ghost and the creature that had pretended to be Mrs. Johnson were not the same.

By the time I got upstairs, the rattling had stopped, and all that was left of the ghost was a very cold spot over the desk that faced the door. When I walked through that spot, I felt like I was back in Alaska tracking the Sasquatch, who had stolen two children from a single mother in a small village near the coast and carried them north.

That was the coldest I'd ever been. Now it was here in the library in one spot. So much for the safety of the library. I wasn't safe anywhere.

The Librarian of The Haunted Library

"I'm just going to make an observation," I said. "Being a librarian is not the safest job in the world."

"I wonder what is the safest job?" the mayor said.

"A lot of them are safe," I said.

"Name one."

"Actuary?" I said.

"I suppose it's possible Lord Blackstone sent it, but the security spells have always been impenetrable to the best of my knowledge. No one, no thing, has ever got past them. Lord Blackstone is a powerful magician, but not that powerful. This is disturbing."

"It's still in the library," I said.

He said they had a team for such situations.

"What kind of team?"

"We have a four-person team. Our science team that deals with demons, evil spirits, difficult ghosts, and any supernatural creatures that cause us problems."

"Who you gonna call?" I said.

"What?"

"Ghostbusters."

"Sounds like that's a movie? I'm not much for movies. I will send the team over."

His window overlooked the square, and I noticed some older ladies coming out into the little park in workout clothes. I thought they were going to do aerobics or yoga.

"This town is not like other towns," I said.

"Every town is a little different."

"Why are we here?" I said.

"I suppose the more philosophically oriented in every town or city on earth ask themselves that question from time to time. Why are we born and why do we die and why are we here in-between?"

He had a point.

"What will the team do exactly?"

"Fumigate the library for dangerous supernatural creatures. I warn you, it doesn't smell good. Like a dead skunk on the side of the road."

The women broke into pairs and the teacher or coach or whatever she was at the front shouted, "Wrestle!"

"I'll send the team over ASAP. Better put the sign up that the library is closed for fumigation today. Luckily, the book club meets tomorrow and not today."

"That is lucky," I said.

They started grabbing each other, going for takedowns. The mayor stood up and looked out the window.

"The wrestling club," he said. "They are early birds."

I left the mayor to finish his meeting and the wrestlers to wrestle in the park. I went to tape a sign on the library door. After I taped the sign to the door, I realized I was still hungry because Mrs. Johnson's eggs and bacon, which I had gobbled down, hadn't really existed. I had been eating air.

I waited for the fumigation team, which I needed to let in. After I did, I walked over to Lucy's café.

It was pretty different from last night. This morning the cafe was filled with people, all the booths taken and most of the tables. It was smokey because of all the breakfasts being cooked. Bacon dominated, but there were a lot of smells floating out from the kitchen. The table where the librarian had died was the only one without customers. It had a reserved sign on it that said RESERVED FOR THE GHOST OF THE DEAD LIBRARIAN.

I sat at the counter where there were still three empty stools.

Lucy was at the cash register. She'd dyed her hair purple. It was white yesterday. Olive had also dyed her hair purple, but some of the black showed through.

The Librarian of The Haunted Library

She passed carrying an impressive number of dishes in her hands, which she dumped carefully into a bus-tub, then grabbed a pot of coffee on a burner and came over to me. I turned up the coffee cup on the saucer in front of the placemat. She poured coffee into it.

"How was your first night in Eden?"

"Eventful," I said.

She saw me adding three sugars and milk but didn't make a comment. I appreciated that.

"Good way or bad way?"

"I had a reoccurring dream in which I'm offered vast riches to destroy the world."

"If you destroy the world," she said, "what good are vast riches?"

"Good point. Also, I had to throw my first cup of coffee on a monster that was trying to kill me before I took even one sip."

"That is bad luck," she said. "I thought monsters weren't supposed to be able to get into the library."

"That's what I was told."

"Barry said it was impossible," she said.

"Barry?"

"The recently deceased librarian."

"Poor Barry," I said.

"Not that poor," she said, her voice sharp but soft in volume.

"What do you mean?"

"Nothing," she said. "Never mind. What are you going to do?"

"The mayor says there's a team that fumigates the library. They're going to try to get rid of her, it."

"Well," she says. "I hope they can. The first cup of coffee is the best of the day."

She went to wait on others. I watched her move around. She seemed to have a kind word for every one of her customers.

"Order up," the cook said.

He was a man with a Pancho Villa mustache. Truth was, he had Pancho Villa's build, too. In pictures, the Mexican general and bandit looked imposing and dangerous. Of course, he often had bandoliers filled with bullets hanging over his shoulders.

A man with long gray hair and a big, bushy gray beard like Rip Van Winkle sat next to me. He had dark, sleepy eyes. I thought he might tell me he had just woken from a thirty-year nap. It was that kind of morning. I looked at his hands. I noticed one of his fingers was missing.

"I see you're looking at my hand and my missing finger."

"No, I wasn't," I lied.

"You've probably noticed that most of the people in town my age and older are missing a finger."

"I haven't been here long," I said.

"But you'll notice and you'll ask yourself why."

"I might," I admitted.

"I could tell you," he said.

"Sure," I said. "I'd like to hear."

Olive stopped by to ask me what I wanted for breakfast. I ordered what I'd ordered the night before, which was pancakes, French toast, eggs, bacon, and sausage.

"Wish I was young enough to eat like that again," Rip Van Winkle said. "Maybe when I get to the other side."

"So, tell me about your missing finger," I said.

"It's not just the finger. It's a story. There's a price."

"What price?"

Rip Van Winkle ordered coffee, toast, eggs over easy, and said, "Put it on his bill."

The Librarian of The Haunted Library

Olive looked at me. I nodded. She poured him coffee, filling the thick pottery cup.

When she was gone, I said, "Let's hear it then."

He told me the story: *This happened in the way back. Two brothers rode into town on the old road that is sometimes there and sometimes not. If it was there, it was dirt, of course. One brother was white and one was black.*

They wore their guns, both of them two pistol gunmen. There was no doubt about their knowing how to use them. They also had Bowie knives and broadside swords in sheaths that hung on straps over their backs. They went to all the houses in town and rounded up the townspeople in the square.

Some people were starting to talk about how they weren't going to let two men tell them what to do. Let alone a Black man and a white man calling themselves brothers. This was another time, you realize. Folks were ignorant and racists. Not like now.

(He paused so we could both smile the sad ironic smiles of men who knew that while now might be better than then, it was not what it should be, not even close.)

So, what the brothers did was shoot all the dogs to make the point that they wouldn't be ignored. That's why the town has no dogs.

It was a sunny, hot day, and we were sweating, all of us. The woods that surrounded Eden often let a breeze slip through, but not on this day. On this day, it was still as a corpse.

The brothers told us they were collectors.

We asked them who they were collectors for and what they were collecting.

"We ain't here to rape any women or chop the private parts off men or burn your pretty little town down," the

57

white brother said. "We're just here to make collections. You give us what we want and we'll be on our way."

They both looked at us like we should know what they wanted.

"'What is it you want?' the mayor said in an accommodating voice. He had been educated back East.

They said they wanted just one finger from each of us. They would prefer a thumb, but any finger would do.

"Course, if you're too frugal and only offer a pinky," the Black brother warned, "We might be tempted to take a second finger."

You understand when I say Black, I'm referring to race and not exact color. He was more the color of mahogany and had smooth skin a woman might envy.

"Why, in god's name, would you need a finger?" the schoolteacher, Mrs. White, asked. She was a strict grammarian with a crisp, precise voice.

"Don't got nothing to do with god," the white brother said.

And the white brother wasn't really white, more tan with a face roughened up by the wind and sun.

"That's our business," the Black brother said. "You just do as you're told. This town would make a pretty fire. Best you pay what's owed."

"If you try to avoid collection," the white brother said, "we will take a whole hand and if you fight us, we'll take your head, and if enough of you fight us, we'll take all your heads."

"You got you ten fingers," the Black brother said. "What we're asking is reasonable".

"Think of it as tithing to your church, schoolteacher," the Black brother said. "Ten is more than anyone needs."

The Librarian of The Haunted Library

The Black brother found this funny and started to giggle, and then the other one giggled.

"What are these dumb asses talking about?" Billy said. Old Billy owned the General Store and had been in the war overseas. I told him to shut up, but he didn't listen. He never listened.

A little mumble of agreement with Billy spread through the crowd. Who did these brothers think they were? The giggling made folks a little bolder than before. It was like it was all a prank.

"This is just a joke?'" the mayor said hopefully. He was still trying to defuse things. He didn't want any fingers cut off, but he didn't want the town killing the brothers, either.

The white brother fired a shot into the air. The brothers stopped laughing.

"I assure you we are serious," the Black brother said.

The town folks were frightened and confused.

"We'll set up over in your little park. Get your doctor to bring antiseptic and bandages. If we get started now, we'll be done before nightfall."

Billy looked around at the rest of us and spit some chewing tobacco on the Black brother's boot.

"Ain't giving you nothing but a beating," Billy said. He looked around at the townspeople. "We'll tar and feather these two and throw them out of town."

We weren't soldiers, though. We were just townspeople.

The white brother, in one smooth movement, reached back and drew his sword and chopped Billy's head off. He wiped the blood off his blade on poor Billy's shirt and put it away.

We lined up in the park. The brothers were done before dark.

Brian Yansky

* * *

"And that is why everyone in our town who was there that day has only nine fingers except for Constance LeBlanc, who had always been a cheapskate and tried to get off with giving a pinky. She has only eight."

Olive brought us our breakfasts. We ate them.

"You probably believe everything happens for a reason, you being a librarian and all," Rip Van Winkle said.

"Not really," I said.

"People always say that, you know. Everything happens for a reason."

"Not a saying I can go along with," I said. "Too many bad things happen to good people. A child gets cancer. Car wrecks. Senseless deaths. Bad weather on wedding days. Situation comedies that should be funny but aren't. You know what I mean."

"Thanks for breakfast," he said.

He stood up.

"Did you know the previous librarian?" I asked.

"I did."

"Olive and he have a relationship?"

"None of my business. What that man did with women, none of my business."

He walked off.

I finished my coffee and paid for our breakfasts at the cash register. I looked around to wave goodbye to Olive but didn't see her. On my way out, I looked for older folks, old like Rip Van Winkle, and saw only one. A woman. She was sitting by herself. I looked at her hands.

"Ms. Le Blanc," I said.

Missing pinky. Missing thumb.

"Do I know you?"

The Librarian of The Haunted Library

"I'm the new librarian," I said. "Just wanted to say hello."

"I'm not paying the fines," she said. "You can just forget it. I already pay taxes. You'll just have to get along without my thirty-five cents."

"Consider it forgiven. I'm having an amnesty week."

"I already pay taxes," she said again.

Just went to show that some people, even if you cut off a finger, weren't about to change.

Chapter Nine

I heard the bells of the café door tinkle behind me. I turned and saw Olive. The tower in the woods had moved. It looked like it was due east of town now.

She said, "Why is a monster after you?"

"I told you. I don't have any idea."

She shook her head. Her eyes drilled into mine. "Don't be dishonest with me. A monster is so desperate to get at you, it breaks into the library. The library is powerful. The monster must really want you dead. I'm asking you why?"

"I already told you I don't know."

"What is it with men? Why can't you just be truthful?"

She looked near tears.

"She said she had orders. Someone ordered her to kill me. That's all I know."

She looked at me. She seemed almost surprised I was there.

"I'm sorry," she said. "I'm just—. I didn't mean to—. I'm upset today and I'm taking it out on you. And you don't even know I'm not usually this way at all."

"Will the librarian please come to the library," a

The Librarian of The Haunted Library

woman's voice, like one speaking through an intercom in a building, said. It was like it came from the heavens. I looked around. I was officially uneasy. Voices did not fall from the sky in my experience.

"Marta," Olive said.

"A goddess?" I said.

"Librarian to the library, please," the voice said.

"Just Marta," Olive said. "Announcer of announcements and news and weather every morning. Special announcements on occasion."

"What occasion?"

"When someone calls her and asks her to make one," she said.

"So, you and the librarian were close?" I said.

"I just knew him from the café, that's all."

"What was he like?"

"You'd better get going," she said. "Sounds like they need you at the library."

She walked back toward the café.

Chapter Ten

A dodo bird was perched on the second-floor balcony of the library. He had a big yellow beak and deep brown eyes. He looked kind.

"All Alone," the dodo bird said in my mind and flew off.

It was the same thing that Big Foot had said. "All alone."

I'd caught up with Sasquatch in Alaska when he was crossing a river. He threw one of the children into it. The water was running, but there were big chunks of ice floating along in the strong current, and I had to make a choice. Sasquatch kept running with the other child under his arm. She looked like a rag doll next to him. The boy in the water was struggling to swim but being pulled under. He was going to die.

I remember standing there for two, maybe three seconds.

Then I jumped off the bridge and rescued the boy in the cold water and built us a fire. We warmed up and slept some and in my sleep, a voice told me that if I opened my eyes, I would see a green door. It was for the Ancients, but I would be allowed to go through it to anyplace I wanted.

The Librarian of The Haunted Library

There were many places I wanted to go. I wanted to see the mother I had never seen give birth to me and see her give me away. I could ask her the question that I had wanted to ask her all my life.

But Big Foot had the girl. She was afraid and alone. She must be cold. Would Big Foot even think to light a fire? He had all that hair to warm him. Or what if he planned on eating her? Would he want her cooked or raw? I couldn't know his intentions.

"I can go anywhere?" I asked the voice.

"Anywhere. Pray to me."

"What god are you?"

"My story is different from your story. Completely different belief systems. It will cost you little to pray to me. But you are rare. The boy of a prophecy. That's worth something. One prayer."

I didn't know what he was talking about, but I knew my prayer was worth a lot to him and that he would use it to do something self-serving in his story. Something probably bad. I prayed to him anyway.

A green door appeared.

I went through the door. On the other side of it, I found the girl in a cave. I didn't see Sasquatch. I got the girl and went back through the door and to the fire.

When I woke, the girl was asleep next to the boy by the fire.

I asked her about Big Foot.

She told me that he wasn't going to eat her, cooked or raw, and he wasn't going to harm her. He just wanted someone to be with him for a while.

* * *

Now that I thought about it, I didn't think Dodo birds could fly.

I walked up to the library.

Chapter Eleven

I went to the library and the four members of the fumigation team were waiting at the door. I let them in. They said they wanted to start with my apartment downstairs. There were two women and two men on the fumigation team. The leader was an older man, probably mid-fifties, named Walter. The women were both from Puerto Rico (Gabriela and Camila), and the other man, Ryan, was from Washington state.

We walked down the stairs to my apartment, and they set up their machine. It was a metal box with four buttons and one dial and a small green screen. It had a curly black cord with a microphone like a police radio. Ryan spoke into it. "Scan for Supernaturals."

"The library attacked a fumigator a generation ago who didn't get the librarian's permission to go into his apartment," Walter said. "All they found of him were his socks."

"Why his socks?" I asked.

"That's your concern?" Gabriela said. "That's what worries you?"

"Troubling," Camila said.

"A legitimate question," Walter said. "You know I knew a man once who refused to wear socks, ever, because his father had never worn socks and his father before him all the way back to the dawn of time, presumably."

"And?" Camila said.

"And what?"

"The connection to the socks left behind in the librarian's apartment."

"I don't believe there is one," Walter said. "Let's look around."

All four members of the fumigation team wore white coats. Three had come to Eden after getting lost hiking. Walter had been working at a secret government facility somewhere out West (he wouldn't say where) and had simply gone for a walk and gotten lost.

"A walk I had taken many times before without incident, well, beyond meeting a bear once," Walt said.

"I've never been sure about that bear," Gabriela said.

"Claims it was a talking bear," Ryan said. "That's the part I'm not sure about."

"You've never met a talking bear?" I said.

"A dancing bear," Ryan said. "I've met a dancing bear. But no, not one who talks."

"You've lived with monks," Walt said to me.

"For a short time," I said.

"And they introduced you to a talking bear?"

"Among other things."

"This bear gave me bad directions," Walter said. "That's how I ended up here. Following the bad directions of a bear."

Everyone had a story about how they got to Eden.

Camila had got lost in a lesbian bar. She said she had been trying to become a lesbian, but was having a hard time with it. She had admitted that it was her anger with men that drove her to women and not desire. It wasn't healthy that she had given into this anger. She'd been arguing with a woman in the bathroom after someone outed her and she'd been stabbed by the woman. Next thing she knew she woke up in the haunted woods.

"A lot of that anger toward men going around in this town," I said.

Gabriela and Camila pointedly looked away. I could have said "man".

Ryan said, "I have a reading, Walter."

"We'd better get to work," Walter said. "These evil spirits won't slay themselves."

"This is a strong reading," Ryan said.

"I recommend you leave us now while we engage with the enemy," Walter said to me.

"I'll be at the front desk if you need me."

I went upstairs to the front desk and what was waiting for me on it was amazing. It was a bowl of mixed fruit. It was exactly what I wanted to eat at that moment, even though I had not been thinking about fruit at all. I was so happy. Sometimes that was all you needed to be happy. A bowl of mixed fruit.

After I finished my fruit, I looked through the computer documents. There were a lot of files and documents on the computer about the library. No internet. No google.

There was a document titled *Notice to the new librarian*. Since that was me, I opened it. According to the information, the books in the library did not always stay in the same place, but a librarian wearing the ring could find what he was looking for by calling the books out.

I read on. I learned that the way to get to the room with the artifacts called the Collection of Curiosities was by pulling out a copy of Sherlock Holmes *Hound of the Baskervilles* and turning to page 42. The bookcase would slide to the side and a green door would be revealed. Then all you had to do was place the ring on the door and it would open.

Hours passed as I read through information about the library.

The fumigation team came walking up the stairs. They looked tired and beat up. Ryan had bruises on his face and a torn lab coat. Camila and Gabriela had burns on their lab coats. Only Walter looked the same as when he'd come in. His hound dog face had the same sad but alert expression.

"We'll need to take the samples back to the lab," he said. "There is something in here we can't catch."

"A demon?" I said.

"Some kind of demon, most likely, but we need more data to be sure what kind."

"Where did you say you were from?" Gabriela asked me.

"Texas originally," I said.

"There will be time later for chit-chat," Walter said. "Now we have work to do."

"The demon can take different forms. It became an old woman from my past," I told them.

"That's what it keeps doing. Shifting away from us by taking new shapes."

"We'll need to make some adjustments and come back later," Walter said. "We're working with a magical creature of advanced skills here."

"Could become almost anyone," Gabriela said. "Tell us about the woman it became."

I told them about Mrs. Johnson.

"You were raised in foster care?" Ryan said.

The Librarian of The Haunted Library

"Yes," I said.

"I was in for a few years. I got adopted when I was six."

"Some do," I said.

And some just watched others get adopted.

"I was lucky," he said.

"I had some good foster parents and some bad ones," I said.

But that wasn't the hardest part. The hardest part was none of them, good or bad, chose me. Except for Mrs. Johnson and she died, maybe because she chose me.

"You boys can talk over your past later," Walter said. "We need to get back to the lab."

"I just hope the evil spirit hasn't laid any eggs," Walter said.

That was the last thing he said. I knew what I'd be thinking about tonight before I fell asleep.

"How did she get in?" Camila said. "That's the real question. Something strange is going on here."

Gabriela said, "A back door of some kind maybe."

"This isn't a computer system or network," Ryan said. "Magic protects the library."

"Maybe magic has a back door, too," Gabriela said.

"Or it could be the former librarian helped someone hack the magic. Someone powerful."

"Anyone in mind?" Gabriela said.

"I think we all know who the number one suspect is," Walter said. "What is more important right now is making the library safe for our new librarian."

"I'd hate to see Death take you today," Gabriela said.

"What day do you have?" I asked her.

At first she pretended she didn't know what I was talking about, but then admitted she had two days from now.

"Probably be a record for shortest employed librarian on record if she gets me today," I said, smiling.

"Not really," they all said at once without any pause, which was disappointing.

Walter said they needed to get back to the lab.

The team left the library. I studied various papers written by former librarians. There were a startling number of librarians. Most of them did not die of natural causes. The causes, in some cases, were extremely unnatural.

The Collection of Curiosities was mentioned in one document. Some curiosities were listed. The knives that were used to stab Julius Caesar, the gun used by the actor John Wilkes Booth to kill Abraham Lincoln, the eating utensils used at the Last Supper.

It was full of strange, beautiful, sad, historical artifacts. How had such curiosities made their way to Eden? I suppose the same way all of us had.

Chapter Twelve

I looked up and out the windows and saw it was dark. The day had slipped away. I got up and stretched. The temperature suddenly dropped. I swung around, expecting Mrs. Johnson. Actually, I was sort of hoping the monster had taken her form again. Even though I knew she wasn't real, it was good to see her.

There was a man standing in front of my desk who looked like Attila the Hun or like I imagined Attila the Hun looked like. Mongolian. Long black hair and beard, savage eyes. He was dressed in animal skins circa 5th century fashion for the Huns. In a major oversight, I had no weapons on me or at my desk. He had two swords strapped over his back and a couple of axes in his belt.

This was not the monster. This was a different ghost. The library was ghost central in Eden.

"What do you think?" he said.

"I think you look like Attila the Hun."

"I do, don't I?" he said. "I hope you are afraid."

"A little," I admitted.

"Good."

He wasn't Attila. I could see past the disguise with my third eye.

"Would you mind not looking like the barbarian?" I said. "Makes me nervous."

He transformed into the most beautiful woman in the world. Or at least she could have been.

"Interesting," she said in a sultry voice. "You seem just as nervous."

"How about the real you?" I said.

He shrugged. He turned into an old man with a mustache and gray hair. I couldn't say who he was, but he had the look of a man who had seen a lot of life even though he was now dead. Anyway, I was sure this was the real him and I tried to memorize his face. One thing I was sure of. His clothes were from an earlier time. Maybe 19th century. His accent was not from back East or the South. I thought most likely Midwestern.

"There's a monster running around," I said. "Have you seen it?"

"As a matter of fact, I have. She threatened me."

"Me too," I said. "Any idea what it is?"

"It's some kind of demon. A servant of the dark forces."

"How many of you are here?"

"I'm not a demon," he said. "I've been haunting the library for years. She is the intruder."

"How did you get here?" I asked.

"I was down in Mexico. In the forest, riding with Pancho Villa and his men. The old bandit left me behind when I got sick. Somehow, I found my way to Eden. The Doc healed me. The town didn't have a librarian at the time. They gave me the job. Seemed a suitable job for someone devoted to words."

"If you're a ghost, why didn't the fumigator get you?"

The Librarian of The Haunted Library

"I know how to make myself scarce when the white coats bring in their machines. I was a librarian, after all."

"You were murdered?"

"Murdered and then imprisoned in the library."

"By who?"

"We can talk about that later."

"How long have you been here?"

"You were in the war, weren't you?" This was a trick question. If he told me which war, I'd have an idea when he was among the living.

"Quid pro quo, my young friend. You tell me something and I'll tell you which war."

"All right," I said. "What do you want to know?"

"I think you've met someone I've met. I'd like to know if I'm right."

"Who?

"Karl."

"Not really," I said.

"What's that mean?"

"I met him in a dream."

He nodded. He said, "The Civil War."

"Any advice for a new librarian?" I said.

"There's a headless woman here. Don't trust headless women."

Chapter Thirteen

The doorbell rang. I went to the front door. There was a woman. She didn't have a head. She held her head in her arms. The head said, "I'd like to talk to you, librarian."

She had an English accent.

"Where are you from?"

"Iowa," she said.

"We're closed," I said. "But I guess I can make an exception for you."

I opened the door. It creaked louder than usual.

"Thank you," she said, coming in. "I am in a bit of trouble."

"I can see," I said.

"I'm not sure what you mean," she said. "I haven't told you about my trouble yet."

I guided her over to the living room. She sat her head on the table by the sofa, where her body took a seat. I sat in the reading chair closest to that side of the sofa.

"I'm here about my daughter," she said.

"Not about—never mind. What about your daughter?"

The Librarian of The Haunted Library

"Why did you think I'd come?"

I was about to say that I thought she'd come because her head wasn't attached to her body, but then I realized that maybe this might be rude. I wasn't sure about the etiquette concerning headlessness. A tricky social situation. I always had trouble with them.

"What about your daughter?" I said.

"She's missing. She went into the woods with three other teenagers and none of them have come back out."

"Your daughter and three other teens are lost in the woods?"

"I wouldn't say lost," she said. "They could just be at the cabin. But you see, they were taken by Cousin Deadeye and kept for a month in his place in the woods recently. No one knows where this place is. We only got them back because Lord Blackstone paid him off. I'm worried that he might take them again."

"Your cousin?"

"Cousin is his first name."

"He's called Deadeye because he's a good shot?"

"He has a dead eye. The one on the left, I believe. It's milky gray. Killed by an angel in battle, he claims."

"He's one of the fallen angels?"

"Don't say that to his face. He says, like many of them do, that he jumped. He still has his wings, but they are black."

"He serves the Dark Lord?" I said.

"Karl."

"*The* Karl?" I said.

"That's the one. It's said that the day of the final battle, Armageddon, approaches. Naturally, heaven's angels have already claimed victory. They tend to do that before a battle has even been fought. Cousin Deadeye is one of

Karl's demon lords. You might call them the aristocrats of hell."

"How long have they been gone?"

"Yesterday and last night and now most of today."

"I don't know the woods well enough to go out at night," I said.

"Of course not," she said. "Only the creatures of the night go out at night. Even Lord Blackstone doesn't, and he is a decorated soldier of the Dark Arts."

"You may not know this, but Lord Blackstone has threatened me," I said.

"He can be a brute. Look at me. Took my head off my body for minor indiscretions. He wants your position. He might take your head, too."

"I'll go to the woods and find your daughter and the others tomorrow," I promised.

I shook her hand. She smiled. She had very white teeth. I told her my name. She asked if there was someone I wanted her to write to if I died unexpectedly in the woods. I said there wasn't.

"I am married," she said. "Right now, I cannot discuss sexual intercourse with you. I am sorry about that. You're a nice-looking boy. Perhaps another time. Thank you for asking."

I was about to tell her I hadn't, but she smiled at me again and I let it go.

"I'll find them," I said.

I dreaded going back into those woods.

"We go to our cabin during the solstice and Halloween and some occasions that require animal sacrifice. Stay the night. You will be quite comfortable there if you make it. There is a crow you may send back with a message if you want to reach me."

"Why would Cousin Deadeye take the teenagers?" I asked.

"You know demons. They've always got some evil plot going. But who kidnaps teenagers? You'd think even demons would know better."

She drew me a map. I was to follow a trail out of town and stay on it all the way to the cabin.

"Do not wander," she said. "There will be dark things hoping that you do."

"How far away is the cabin?"

"That depends on you," she said.

"Distance is distance," I said.

"Some say so. But the trail is different for everyone."

"I'll find your daughter, Lady Blackstone," I said.

"You can call me Catherine when we're alone. I think we will be lovers one day. If we're making love and you're calling me Lady Blackstone, I will feel matronly."

"I'll remember that," I said.

"Catherine is not my name, of course. My secret name is very long. Like a password."

She picked up her head. It was a lovely head. Thick black hair, a pretty mouth, big hooded brown eyes, makeup perfectly applied. She had not let herself go simply because her head was separated from her body.

"I'll leave tomorrow after my shift," I said.

"This is an emergency. My daughter's life might be at risk."

"I understand," I said. "But I'm the librarian first. Maybe you should talk to the constable."

"He won't go into the woods, the coward."

I'd been reading the library rules. I could only miss opening the library three times before I would be fired, except in situations beyond my control. This one wasn't one of those.

"Eleven," I said.

I let her out. The sun was going down.

I knew she might be setting me up for her husband or herself or maybe even Cousin Deadeye. Still, I had to go. It was my job. I took work seriously. I also took demon lords seriously, especially ones close to Karl.

Chapter Fourteen

Had I met Cousin Deadeye? Maybe. It was nearly two years ago that I met the demon I thought might be Cousin Deadeye.

I came to a little town, Hawthorne, Vermont, because I'd been directed by the voice in a dream to go there and find a woman in a bakery crying. Even before I found a bakery in the town, I could see right away there was trouble. A coffin was propped up in a store window. Inside was a middle-aged male corpse with a sign hung round his neck and the word *Rapist* written in magic marker. Many people seemed to be hurrying around town with frightened looks, like they were in a rush to get somewhere safe, but they weren't sure where that was.

I went to the bakery I'd seen in my dream.

A woman whose name was Mustang Sally was sitting at a table crying when I opened the door. The bells on the door tinkled. She wiped her tears with her sleeve and said, "I'm sorry. Excuse me for just one second."

She disappeared in the back. I sat at a table by the big picture window. When she came back, she'd washed her face and composed herself. She even tried to smile. I ordered an elephant ear and coffee, three sugars and cream. She got them for me.

"On the house," she said.

"I'd like to pay," I said. "I know you must be struggling with what's going on here."

Most of my callings involved people who could not pay me, but from time to time they involved people with some money and occasionally people with a lot of money. They paid me for my help. It always seemed to work out that I had enough to live on, but not much to spare.

Mustang Sally wouldn't let me pay, anyway. She was insistent and stubborn.

"Someone has come to town?" I guessed. That was what I saw in the townspeople. I'd seen it before. Someone, like a virus, had infected the town.

She said everything had changed when a man calling himself Blackheart had come to town. It had only been one week ago, though it seemed like a lifetime. She didn't know how that had happened. Her own brother had been killed in a knife fight. He'd never been in a fight in his life before this past week.

"We're just normal folks. He showed up, this man, and everything changed."

"Blackheart?" I said.

"Man is aptly named, but my guess is it's more descriptive than authentic."

"What's he done?" I asked.

"That's the terrible thing. He hasn't done anything. Just talks to people. But it's how he talks to them."

Mustang Sally took me over to talk to the sheriff in a little office.

"Man hasn't done anything illegal," he said. "Folks are just looking for a scapegoat."

I asked him what crimes had happened, and he told me. He probably wouldn't have, but I tapped the back of his hand three times and spoke to him in soft truth-teller whispers.

A boy had stabbed his mother and said he'd done it because she had bullied him all his life. Two old friends got into a fight in the park. It was over politics. They had voted for the same party all their lives, but they got in an argument about candidates and beat each other so badly they both ended up in the county hospital. A husband and wife had nearly killed one another over burnt toast. They were both in the hospital, too.

"All these things happened after Darkheart came to town?" I asked the sheriff.

"It's an evil world," the sheriff said. "But we ain't arresting someone for people's own weaknesses."

I asked him with another truth-teller whisper if he'd ever heard of the Satan Society.

"Damn right I worship the devil. My whole family does. We are devout. We have faith that the world will soon be just what we want. No more pretending. It's going to be hideous. Praise the Dark One."

I couldn't expect any help from him. In fact, he might get to thinking after I left that I needed to be stopped if I was going to get in the way. I locked him up in a jail cell and planted a false memory in his mind of him getting tired and locking himself in a cell to catch some sleep.

Then I spent the next couple of hours going around town and talking to people and letting them hear what Darkheart said. Then I went to Darkheart's room in the only hotel in town.

"You're here to interfere in my work?" he said, asking me to come in and have a drink.

"You've done enough," I said.

I turned down the drink. He had one anyway.

"You're like the little boy with his finger in the dike. You can't stop what's coming. This world wants us to win."

"I don't think so. Your whispers have been exposed."

That was what I'd done. I made the whispers he'd been leaving around town loud, and when people heard them spoken out in the open, they heard the lie in them and in the voice.

All of his lies began to be heard by all of those who had given into jealousy or anger and those who were working up to it. How had they been deceived? How had they been so stupid? Some of them had acted badly and some had been victims. Most of them were ashamed and angry.

"They're coming for you," I told him.

"Are they?"

"They've got shotguns and pitchforks."

"Old school," he said.

"That's why you won't win."

"It won't change anything," he said. "I'll just find another town."

I shrugged. "Some day you'll run out of towns."

"I would have already killed you, but Lucifer has forbidden it. He still thinks you might be the chosen one. I know better. Someday soon, I will come for you."

"I'll be waiting," I said.

"Someday very soon," he whispered, and I felt the fear take hold of me and I had to fight it to keep from running from the room.

We heard them downstairs in the hotel lobby. They came marching up the stairs. Darkheart was gone by the time they got to the room. He'd left out the window. I couldn't get to the window fast enough to see him go, but I thought, off in the distance, I caught a glimpse of a creature flying, a black-winged creature. In a second, it had disappeared and I could never be sure I'd really seen it.

Now I was sure. Dead eye. Black wings. Cold heart. I couldn't deny that his hypnotic whispers were like my own. I'd never called them magic, but if they were, then what kind of magic were they that an angel with black wings used them, too?

Chapter Fifteen

I went over to Lucy's after my meeting with Lady Blackstone. It was nearly time for the café to close. I asked Olive if it was too late for a burger and fries. She said it was too late for anyone but the new librarian.

"My lucky day then," I said.

When she brought the order, she sat down at my booth. I told her about Lady Blackstone, who had just visited me carrying her head.

"She's a formidable lady," she said.

"That must be a very special blade," I said.

I took a bite of my hamburger.

She shrugged. "Lord Blackstone is a powerful magician. Ever met one?"

"A few," I said. "We had one in the circus I travelled with for a time."

"What were you?" she said. "Fortune teller?"

"Crew. Set up and tear down," I said, "and occasionally filled in on the trapeze when Carlos and Dido got in a marital spat and couldn't work together."

"Were you good?"

"I never dropped Dido."

"I'm sure she appreciated that," she said.

"I did help a magician once in Seattle. He was being run out of business by a new conglomerate, Magical Incorporated. They tried to recruit him and when he refused, they tried to run him out of business by burning his store down, and then, when that didn't work, killing his familiar. One of the magician thugs tried to turn him into a dumpster."

"You stopped him?"

"Stopped isn't quite how I'd put it. I convinced the thug magician, with persuasive whispers, to reverse the spell. He turned it on himself and was turned into a dumpster. People might still be throwing trash into him today."

"Those big magic companies can be ruthless," she said.

"Why'd Lord Blackstone cut off her head?" I asked.

"She cheated on him."

"With who?"

"Most of the men in town."

Pancho Villa's twin came out from the kitchen and poured himself a cup of coffee.

"What's going on out here?" he asked.

"We're talking about how Lady Blackstone slept with most of the men in town."

"She ain't slept with me yet. And now it's too late. I ain't sleeping with no headless women. I've got standards."

"You'd sleep with her in a heartbeat," Olive said.

"Damn," he said, shaking his head at himself, "you're right."

He went back through the swinging doors.

"The librarian?" I said.

She shrugged.

"That's a yes?" I said.

"I guess," she said. "Their daughter begged Lord Blackstone to make her mother whole again, and he compromised. He said he would reattach her head if she could go one year without cheating on him. She has four days to go and she'll be whole again."

"Why didn't he just divorce her?"

"They'd have to split up their possessions. All their poisons. All their potions. Their books on black magic. And the town is small. I think they might actually care for each other, too. I'm not sure. They're both excellent liars."

She said she needed to set up for tomorrow's breakfast. She went and locked the door; while she set up, I finished my hamburger and fries.

Olive came back to the table after a while. "You want to go over to The Bar? Have a drink?"

"Sure," I said.

We went to The Bar. It was small but cozy. Red leather booths, a few tables, and a pool table in back. Room at the bar to stand and four stools. Olive and I took two of them.

There were about twenty customers. It was dark, just lamp light from the tables and a fluorescent lamp over the pool table. A woman laughed from back behind the pool table. She sounded like Julia Roberts's in *Pretty Woman*. I was sort of a connoisseur of bars. Some nights a bar could be the best place to be and some nights the worst and some nights the best and the worst at the same time. This one was comfortable, which was my favorite kind. What I couldn't abide was a bar that was neutral and had no personality.

Three older customers stood at the end, looking like they'd just woke up from a dream. Nine fingers.

One of them with only two teeth, the ones Bugs Bunny so prominently displayed, said, "I know who you are."

I thought that he was going to tell me something I didn't really want to know.

He said, "You're the new librarian."

"Right," I said, relieved. "That's who I am."

"I'll be over tomorrow. I need some light reading. Maybe Dante's *Inferno*. You can give me the inside scoop."

He walked away. We sat on stools at the end of the bar. I noticed Olive had delicate hands, long fingers, and narrow shoulders.

"What was that about?" Olive asked.

I shrugged. "People seem to think librarians know all kinds of stuff."

"You want a gin and tonic?" she said.

The bartender, a handsome man with a scar that went across his neck from ear to ear, came up to us. Olive made signs in the air. The bartender nodded.

"He's deaf?" I said.

A man about three stools over held up his napkin. He'd written WHISKEY on it.

"We think he was in the mafia," Olive whispered. "All he'll say is he was a cleaner for the Italians in New York City back in the day when the Italians were in control. Doc says someone cut out his tongue."

If there was a pattern to who ended up in Eden, I couldn't see it. Yet.

"How did you get here?" I asked Olive.

"My parents. We were hiking. We got lost."

"How old were you?"

"I was ten. Me and my dad got separated from my mother."

"In the woods? In these woods?"

"I think so. It's hard to say where the woods we were in became these woods. But my father seems certain we were in the haunted woods."

"You haven't seen her since?"

"No."

The bartender set down bar napkins and then the gin and tonics. His movements were quick and efficient. Olive made a sign for, I assume, thank you. I made the same sign. I hoped, for several reasons, I wasn't saying *Meet me out back for a quicky*.

"You don't know if she's alive?"

"No."

I said I was so sorry. She looked close to tears. But she did not live close to tears. She was not one of those people.

"Tell me about you," she said.

I knew what she was doing, but I didn't blame her. To lose your mother that way and to not know if she was alive or dead, that was hard. I was used to losing people. I was moved up and down the Texas coast in foster care so often I made sure I never needed more than my backpack and a pillowcase to carry all I owned.

"What do you want to know?" I asked.

"You don't know who your mother or father is?"

"No," I lied. Well, half-lied. I had no idea who my mother was, although if there was a prophecy and if it was the one I thought it might be, I'd know her profession. I had an idea about my father. I might as well admit it. I had an idea.

"You were born in an orphanage?"

"I was dropped off in an orphanage by someone."

"Where were you born?" I asked her.

The Librarian of The Haunted Library

The bartender reached up and caught a dart whose point would have been buried in his ear. One of the old men with nine fingers came up.

"My aims off a little tonight, Henry. Apologies."

The bartender handed him the dart and nodded. Maybe he could read lips or maybe he just knew what the old man would say if he could hear him.

"Boulder," she said. "My father lived there. My mother was passing through. Hitchhiking like you."

"He picked her up?"

"Yes," she said. "Have you ever tried to find your parents?"

"No," I said.

"Never?"

"I sort of look for her sometimes. My mother. I have this, I don't know what to call it, feeling that if I see her I'll know it's her. So, I look sometimes. Like on a crowded street or at a concert or something."

"No crowded streets here."

"Did they try to find your mother?" I asked her. I suppose my voice was soft or the noise in the bar had got louder.

"What?" she said.

I leaned toward her and smelled her perfume, something cool on a hot day. I asked her again.

"My father talked to powerful people like the mayor and Lord Blackstone and the Librarian and tried to get their help."

"What about a search party?"

"The Librarian at the time took my father out into the woods twice. The second time, they almost died. Pygmy headhunters. "

"Not, I assume, someone trying to find them a job."

"Little men and women with spears that enjoy shrinking heads if they can find them. Apparently, they can find them in the woods attached to living bodies, which they turn into dead ones before they shrink the heads."

"At least they're humane headhunters," I said.

"My father said they had trees full of heads hanging from the branches."

My promise to go into the woods seemed even more foolish in the light of pygmy headhunters. What other things lived or lurked in those woods? I knew one—Cousin Deadeye.

When the bartender came by, I put up two fingers and he nodded. Anyway, I'd promised I'd go. I had this thing about breaking promises.

"When I was out in those woods last time," I said, "I heard whispers. I knew something was coming for me, waiting for its chance."

"I guess it didn't get it," she said.

I shrugged. "Sunrise stopped it. Odd thing was the sun had been hidden until then. The trees must have thinned out, only I don't remember that happening."

"Odd things seem to happen to you," she said.

"Your father was captured by headhunters," I reminded her.

"True."

The bartender served us two more drinks. I took a long swallow, still thinking about those whispers.

"How old are you?" she asked me.

"Twenty-eight. You?"

"Twenty-seven," she said.

"Why does Lord Blackstone want to be the librarian all of a sudden, do you think?"

"He's always wanted to be the librarian."

"But he didn't act on it, right? After the previous librarian's death, he came to collect it, like a prize."

"Some people say he's been waiting for a specific time. The Christians in town think when he becomes librarian, it will be the End of Days, the days leading up to the final battle, Armageddon. Some who aren't Christian think so, too. They just think that the battle isn't between good and evil exactly, but between two groups of angels that have been at war for eons."

"What do you think?" I asked her.

She shrugged. "Either way, I don't think it's going to be good for humans. Did you dream about Eden? Hear that voice you told me about? Is that why you came here? Some kind of mission?"

"No," I said. I didn't tell her I'd dreamed about the clown. I don't know why.

"I'm not sure the mayor can hold Lord Blackstone off twice. You'd better stay alive."

"I'll do my best," I said.

"You do know you can't trust Lady Blackstone, right?" Olive said.

"The ghost of the library told me not to trust headless women," I said. "Are there others in town?"

She shook her head. "Barry told me there was no ghost."

"The former librarian. You knew him pretty well?"

"Like I said before, just from the cafe. He ate there most days. Like you will. One of the regulars."

"I think I have to go find the teenagers. What are the chances teenagers in a haunted wood won't get in trouble?"

"So, there's really a ghost," she said.

"A writer, I think. He fought in the Civil War."

"Did Mark Twain fight in the Civil War?"

"I don't think so," I said. "He does sort of look like Mark Twain, though."

She smiled sadly. "The ghost is right about not trusting Lady Blackstone. It could be a trap. You go into the woods and you don't come back and Lord Blackstone takes your position. Lady Blackstone could have made some kind of deal with him."

"The thought occurred to me," I said.

"Take the Librarian's sword."

"The what?"

"There's a sword from the special collection. Take it."

"I don't know how to use a sword," I said.

"The first librarian is supposed to have acquired it from King Arthur. That's the story. Anyway, it's magical. It will help you use it."

"Really?"

"Magical, yes. Maybe not Excalibur though. He said he believes it was the sword of a famous knight of the crusades named, I think, Godfrey of Bouillon. Anyway, take it."

I said I would because a magical sword that I didn't know how to use was better than no sword at all.

Olive asked me to walk her home. It was not much of a walk, all of two blocks down Main street, but to be fair, there was nowhere in Eden that was much of a walk. She lived with her father in a big Victorian house that sat on a weedy corner lot. It had a wrought-iron fence around it that could use some work.

We stopped at the gate.

I hadn't noticed the house before. I was beginning to think that the town was like the tower, which seemed to move from place to place. It did seem like I saw a few houses and buildings today that I hadn't seen yesterday.

The Librarian of The Haunted Library

Today, I didn't see the church when we walked by the square.

"A haunted house?" I said.

"I suppose you could call it that," she said. "It has a dead person living in it."

We stood close to each other at the gate. I wanted to kiss her. I was leaning toward her. She was leaning toward me. But for some reason, she pulled away, or maybe I pulled away. We couldn't quite connect. The wind picked up and a murder of crows passed by overhead caw-cawing. They spoiled the mood.

"Good night," I said.

"Good night."

When I got back to the library, I stepped into the main room and flipped on the light switch. I jumped back because the ghost was about three feet in front of me.

"You go out into the woods and there's a good chance you won't come back, my friend." He was smoking a cigar, and he blew out a mouthful of smoke.

His mustache was, I thought, like Mark Twain's. The man wasn't wearing a white suit, though.

"Have you seen something?" I asked. Dead people sometimes saw the future.

"I know over fifty librarians have died in the woods. That's what I have seen."

"Been killed, you mean," I said.

"Disappeared," he said. "It may be you can free me of this prison. Would you do that if you could?"

"I think so," I said. "As long as you're not a serial killer or something terrible."

He shrugged. Which could have meant *what an absurd notion* or *I'm not going to say one way or another*. There must be an article somewhere on shrug interpretation. Note to self: find one and read it.

I was going out into those woods to find those kids because they were in danger. You'd think I was trying to make up for something because I was trying to make up for something. I knew I wasn't alone in this, but it still made me feel lonely when I thought about all the things I needed to make up for.

Chapter Sixteen

I woke up late and had to run upstairs to the front desk without a shower or even a cup of coffee. It was 9:04 when I opened the front door. A man in a long black coat wearing a fedora hat came through it. His hair was gray.

"You're late," he said.

I walked back over to my desk.

"Sorry," I looked at his hands. Five fingers on the left and four fingers on the right. What did those brothers do with all those fingers? I really would like to know.

"I used to work for the government," he said.

"Doing what?" I asked.

He shook his head. "Can't say."

"FBI?"

"Can't say."

"CIA?"

"Can't say.

"Were you in the X-files?" I said.

"That's very funny," he said. "Open on time. You'll get a

bad reputation. You don't want to get a bad reputation in Eden."

I almost told him that I would lie awake worrying about my reputation, but then I remembered I had a rule not to be snarky before my first cup of coffee. He did strike me as someone who it might be worth breaking the rule for in the future, but I sat down quietly at my desk.

He went over to the living room area. It had a sofa, chair and coffee table. On the coffee table was a newspaper. He picked it up and sat down on the sofa. He opened the paper. It was *The New York Times*. I couldn't see the date.

"Is that today's?" I asked him.

"Why would I read yesterday's paper?" he said.

He had me there.

"But how could today's paper get here?"

"You're the librarian," he said. "You tell me."

I thought about it and I thought that things worked differently here than elsewhere and I didn't know what that meant, but I'd put off trying to come up with a meaning for now because I had a more pressing problem. I was about to go out into the woods. And the woods were deadly and creepy. And, apparently, teeming with pygmy headhunters.

I needed to protect myself. I needed some bug repellent.

Marta gave the morning announcements. The sound of her voice was piped into the library. She predicted the weather would be like yesterday and tomorrow. She went through several news items. Charlie Bird had lost his pig Bernard again. That pig was a wanderer. "If anyone sees him, please bring him back to Charlie's." Televisions had come on in the middle of the night and were still working. "Watch your morning shows while you can. There will likely be a short window of watch time. Storms are moving

The Librarian of The Haunted Library

in down below." She went on for another five minutes. She even mentioned me. She said the librarian was about to go into the woods to rescue some teens who had not returned yesterday, and then she named the four teens, including the Blackstone's daughter, Diana. She said that I should be in the prayers of those who prayed to the god of their choice or whatever supernatural entity they preferred. "We all wish him well and if we don't see him again, we want him to know that his short time as librarian was appreciated. Also, congratulations to the winner of the pool if there is a winner."

I needed a cup of coffee. I supposed there were rules against drinking coffee in the library. But then I realized I was the librarian and so made the rules and I was very much against such a rule. I went to my apartment and made a cup of coffee and brought it upstairs to my desk.

"You can't have that in here," Mr. Government worker said.

"New rule," I said. "I can."

"You think you can just make up new rules?" he said.

"I think so," I said.

"There are channels," he said. The Government worker stood up. He looked angry. "Government channels. Red tape. Blue tape. All kinds of tape. You need to get a new rule approved by the proper people in the proper channels, and only then can your documents work themselves up the chain until the signature needed signs with the needed signature. Only then can you have new rules."

His voice had got louder and louder during this speech.

"Or I can just bypass all that."

He was spitting with rage then. "Bypass, bypass, are you insane? I will report this to the council. I will have you disbarred."

"I thought that was for lawyers," I said.

"You do not respect authority."

He had me there. I had what I considered a healthy suspicion of it and rules in general, and the people who made them in particular. Not that the world didn't need some rules, like the rule of law, for instance. But quite a few rules were made by someone hoping to use the rule to benefit themselves, and even a good rule could sometimes be applied in a bad way. Rules should be viewed with suspicion first and acceptance second.

At ten o'clock, a book club came in. There were five older ladies, one younger one, and a very tall man. They were reading *The Southern Book Club's Guide to Slaying Vampires*. I'd read that book. I liked that book. One of the book club's members had a cousin who he said had gone through the change when she was going through the change.

"Which was harder?" one woman said.

That got chuckles from all of them and a polite smile from the younger woman and the tall man, neither of who, obviously, had been through the change.

The group discussed their experiences with vampires and it was a bit disturbing that they had all had encounters with the blood drinkers or had known someone who had. I had had encounters with one once, but my life was not normal. They all looked normal enough, but one of them had confessed to slaying a neighbor who happened to be a vampire and had attacked her dog, a Maltipoo, named Sweetie.

"Drove a stake right into his heart. You don't mess with someone's dog. You just don't."

Near closing at eleven, Ryan came in. He said that they had analyzed the poison that killed the librarian for Doc, and it was the same one that did in Socrates, hemlock. Very common in the woods around the town, so that was no help in narrowing down suspects.

"Just about anyone could have picked it," he said.

"All right."

"And we think your evil spirit is a ghoul. A demon but one with a specialization."

"In what?"

"Have you had any experience with ghouls?" he asked.

I thought for a second. "There was this teacher I had in sixth grade, Mr. Fry. He had a sort of ghoulish face. He had a way of looking at you that always made you think he was looking away from you. I think he was cross-eyed."

"They like to eat people," Ryan said.

"As far as I know, Mr. Fry never ate anyone."

"They're kind of known for it," Ryan said. "They have big appetites."

"And that's their specialty?"

"That sounds like a specialty to you?

"Not really. More a culinary choice."

"The specialty is information. They're dealers in information."

"Like spies?"

"Sort of like spies, except they don't work for a government or anyone really except themselves. Which means the highest bidder. If someone wants to know something that no one else knows, a ghoul is a good hire."

"I did not know that."

"The story is that they know the way to Heaven and they get up close to the walls and ease-drop on angels."

"I guess you'd hear some important things if you could do that."

"Walt believes that ghoul scientists have really made some excellent listening devices in the last decade."

"There are ghoul scientists?"

"I'm just saying that's what Walt thinks. They could just have great hearing. That's another thought."

"How'd he or she get into the library?"

"Ghouls can be both he and she, I think. Since they are excellent at gathering information, maybe he or she or they learned some way. The unusual thing is for the ghoul to be an assassin."

"He or she or they seemed pretty experienced," I said. "Putting them aside for a moment, the real question is who hired the ghoul and why?"

"Could have made some deal with Lord Blackstone," Ryan said.

"The thought crossed my mind," I said.

"But you don't think so?"

"I wouldn't rule it out."

"Walter thinks the ghoul is hiding in a book. Any ghouls in books come to mind."

"Maybe *A Thousand and One Nights*," I said. "What would it be like to stand outside heaven and eavesdrop on angels?"

"Too much for me," Ryan said. "I'd prefer a drink over at The Bar."

"Thanks for the information," I said.

"We'll have to get a beer at The Bar sometime," Ryan said. "Talk about orphanage life."

"Sure," I said, though I dreaded being told how Ryan had been adopted. It seemed like orphans who got adopted always had to tell you how they got adopted and the actual experience of being chosen. When I listened, it just brought back all the times I hadn't been chosen. I didn't like that it bothered me. I should have been harder by now, but that was the thing about childhoods; they followed you all the way into adulthood and probably all the way to the grave, a flock of memories fluttering over you as you took your last breath.

What a strange thing life was.

At eleven, I closed up the library.

I considered going over to the café for lunch before I went looking for the Blackstone's daughter and the other missing teens, but instead I went down to my apartment and hunted for food. Though now that I thought about it, I suppose I was technically gathering. I didn't find anything.

I went over to the bookcase and pulled out *The Hound of the Baskervilles* and turned to page 42. The bookcase slid to the side and revealed a green door, like the one in my dream for the Ancients, whoever they were. I opened it with the librarian's ring.

The light was dimmer than I would have liked in the room where the Collection of Curiosities was. The room was square, about the size of a large bedroom. But I could see that there were many rooms, one after another, like boxy storage units. They stretched farther than I could see through the open doorways lined up so that with the proper equipment, binoculars or a telescope, you could likely see all the way to a far wall.

The sword, in a sheath, was being held by an empty (I hoped) suit of armor. If this were a certain kind of movie, the suit of armor would have someone inside it. A mummy or some kind of dead spirit not very happy about being woken from a very long nap.

"Anyone in there?" I said, tapping on the helm.

No response. Not surprising. If there was someone in there, they'd have to be a little dense to answer.

I circled around and came up from behind the armor and grabbed the sword. No attack from the armor. I pulled the sword out of its sheath. It was a beauty. Could have been Excalibur. Probably not, but could have been.

I was tempted to walk through a few rooms in the Collection of Curiosities, but there were teenagers out in a haunted wood and I knew what I had to do. I went upstairs. I locked up the library and went down to the little grocery store half a block off Main. I asked the owner, a dark-skinned man of Italian descent I thought, if I could run a tab and he said that anything I bought would automatically go on the mayor's tab. So, I bought a small backpack I could put over my shoulder and some potato chips and cheese and apples and a bottle of water.

"You sure about this?" the owner of the store said. "The woods, they are deadly."

He shivered.

"Not one bit," I said.

"I was one of them who not find Eden for a week," he said. "Still have the nightmares."

"You have a later date in the pool?" I asked.

"That is not why I'm warning you," he said. "You do not understand the woods."

"What's your number?"

"Seven days," he said.

"I'll do my best to make it back," I said.

"I'll be rooting for you."

Chapter Seventeen

I walked the trail, following the map. The woods were thick. The leafy trees hid the sun and the light it provided. The birds in the trees, their varied songs and squawking and cawing were the woods equivalent of a busy New York street. I heard monkeys chattering behind the birds. I came to a diverging of trails that was not on the map that Lady Blackstone had given me. I took this as a bad sign. If she wanted to get me lost and murdered by one or many of the dark things in the woods, bad directions would be a good strategy.

I stayed to the right, hoping it was right. After another twenty feet, there was another diverging of trails, also not on the map. I stayed to the right, hoping again it was right. Then I came to a third diverging of paths. I decided to follow Frost's advice and take the path less taken, which was to the left.

After about twenty minutes, I came to a small clearing, and I saw the tower far off, higher up the mountain than yesterday. Nearly to the top. I thought I saw something flying over it. Eagles? Too big for eagles. Dragons? Dragons in woods. What could go wrong?

I was paying attention to the tower, so I didn't notice the wild boar running across the clearing until he was about thirty feet away. I stayed perfectly still, but that didn't seem to fool him. I suppose he relied more on smell than sight.

I tried to whisper to him that what was in front of him was a grizzly bear, but I knew this was unlikely to slow him one bit. I was too far away. He had a primitive mind.

The forest went dark. I thought maybe I did it somehow. Then I thought this was one of those cases where two unrelated events seemed related. Like someone walking under a ladder and then being struck by a piece of falling cosmic debris. Unless the two were actually related in ways I couldn't see because of my limited sight.

Then I thought maybe the forest was dark only in my head. I could hear the boar rushing toward me. I felt fear crawl up the back of my neck like an insect. The boar's snorting got louder as he got closer. I crouched, moving the right foot out in a fighting stance. I'd just got my arms up when the lights came back on.

Unfortunately, the boar with giant tusks was on top of me by then. I grabbed the sword and swung it around, but I was too slow. The tusks were about to spear me. I was about to have two very large holes.

The beast stopped in its tracks when it saw the sword. It was immediate. It was still a miracle he didn't gore me. The tusks were touching my chest. It bowed down. I waved the sword, which the boar was careful not to look at.

I started to back away, but then I stopped. Where was I going to go? Something about the boar's face made me think he might be intelligent.

"Do you speak English?" I asked the boar.

"A little," he said.

"Can you point me toward Lord Blackstone's cabin?"

"I'm not much for pointing. You need fingers for that."

"Right. Sorry. Maybe you could just nod."

He nodded to the right.

"Why didn't you kill me?" I asked and immediately regretted bringing up the subject.

"Sword."

"What about the sword?"

"It is the sword in the stone."

"Excalibur?"

"I can smell it. I can smell across the centuries. King Arthur's sweat."

"Really?"

"And now I also smell the witch. I'm out of here."

"What witch?"

"Of the woods. One eye. Run human."

He took off running.

A witch, who did in fact have a patch over one eye, wearing a pointy black hat, appeared in the clearing. She was on a hovering broomstick about six feet off the ground. She wore a black dress and black shoes. Old school. My guess was she hadn't updated her look for centuries.

"You are off the magic path in my woods," she said and shook a finger (crooked, of course) at me.

"Sorry about that."

"My woods," she said. "Unprotected and off the magic path. That is a big mistake."

"I heard you, and I'm not exactly unprotected."

"You look unprotected to me. Lost the path, didn't you?"

"I purposely wondered off it," I lied. "And I have a sword called Excalibur."

She laughed. "You think I haven't heard that before? I have a sword. You think you're the first man to talk to me about his sword?"

"What? No. A real sword. Excalibur," I said.

"I will turn you into a toad."

"That's a little old-fashioned, don't you think?" I said. "I suppose you still cook children in a wood stove, too."

She frowned. Her brow definitely furrowed.

"You'd probably have me microwave them. The fact is, they just don't taste as good that way. Get kind of rubbery. And as for turning you into a toad, what's wrong with that?"

"Nothing."

She raised a hand as if to slap me with a spell. She held back for some reason.

"Enlighten me. What do witches turn people into now?"

"Maybe zombies. Something like that."

"Hmph," she said.

"Anyway," I said. "Back to my sword. All I had to do was raise it and that boar bowed down. Can you imagine what would happen if I gave it a swing? Excalibur. This is the greatest sword of all time."

"You don't have Excalibur."

"The big pig smelled King Arthur's sweat."

"Show me."

I reached back for the sword. She raised her hand in a defensive position.

I pulled it out. It was a good-looking sword. The light from the sun glinted off it into the witch's eyes.

She looked at me and at the sword. "You can pass, but not because you have that sword."

"Because you like me?"

"I don't," she said.

"A little bit?"

"Go now before I change my mind."

"Thank you," I said. "You haven't by any chance seen four teenagers, have you?"

"No," she said, looking away.

"Where are they?"

"How should I know?" She was still looking away.

I raised the sword.

"Fine," she said. "In the cabin last I saw."

"You put them there?"

"Let's just say they're under house arrest."

"Why?"

"I'm a wicked witch."

"Why lock them in a house?"

"I didn't have anything for dinner. I thought I might make a stew later."

"Out of teenagers?"

"Not just teenagers. Onions, carrots, green beans, spinach and potatoes."

"Wouldn't the meat be kind of tough?"

"All the witch foodie magazines advise teenagers over fat little children these days. Lean meat. Better for you."

"I'm taking them back to Eden."

"Probably for the best. Someone would make a big deal about these teenagers. I'd have to falsify my report to the town. I'm just not as good at subterfuge as I once was."

"What report?" I asked.

"Each month, I have to report evil things I've done that might negatively affect the town. If those kids die, then the town will take action against me. But they won't because you're going to save them, so it's a win-win. I get to do some evil, blow off a little steam, live my passion, and you get the teenagers back. Though their parents might not be all that happy about it before long. I have a teenage girl myself."

She flew off. I walked on.

"Stay out of my woods, librarian," she shouted as she passed out of sight.

I walked on, keeping my eyes open. A good thing too, because I came to some strange soil that looked suspiciously like quicksand. I put one foot in it before I'd fully comprehended the significance of quick in the word quicksand. The pit grabbed hold and sucked me down.

I drew the sword and chopped at an exposed tree root.

"Ouch," a voice shouted.

"Sorry," I said.

"Sorry? You chopped off my root."

I grabbed hold of the root.

"No choice," I said.

I was able to pull myself out, one difficult handhold at a time. The tree kept telling me how much it hurt and he expected to be compensated.

Once I got out, I thanked him.

"Not good enough," the tree said. "I want you to sing me a song."

"I'm a terrible singer."

"I'll be the judge of that. Sing."

The only song that came to mind was Alice Cooper's "Schools Out.

"Stop, stop," he said when I had hardly got to the chorus.

"You are a terrible singer."

"Told you."

I found a piece of dead wood and used my sword to cut words into it.

"What do you think you're doing?" the tree said.

"Making a warning sign."

"You can't do that."

"I don't want anyone else to stumble into the quicksand," I said.

"And what am I supposed to do?"

"Excuse me?"

"Go somewhere else to get a little entertainment? Did you ever think of that? Did that ever cross your mind that it might be the only entertainment I have, watching people getting stuck in quicksand?"

"I have to say that it didn't cross my mind."

"Just as I thought. No one ever thinks about how dull it is to never go anywhere. They just say, beautiful tree, or lovely forest, never for one second imagining how tiring the same view gets."

"I'm sorry," I said.

"You can repay me by throwing that sign into the quicksand."

I couldn't do that and I told him I couldn't, and he cursed me.

I walked on. Not much else to do when a tree is cursing you. One good thing, he couldn't follow.

Chapter Eighteen

I walked on in the direction the witch had pointed, which seemed like the right direction for me. That was important because if you took directions from a one-eyed witch, you had to be prepared for disappointment. I wandered around for a few hours before I met a crow named Leonard who gave me more directions. I'd asked him, of course. He didn't just fly up to me.

"Do all animals and trees talk in this haunted woods?" I said.

"Not all crows or all trees," he said. "In fact, there are relatively few of us in the whole woods. It's interesting you happened to find us."

"I'm good at finding things," I said. "The cabin is the exception."

"Maybe there's a reason."

I asked him what, and he shrugged. A crow was a good shape for shrugging. I think I may have understood that shrug. It was a "how should I know I'm a crow," shrug.

"Any idea how far it is?" I said.

"About ten minutes as the crow flies," he said and flew off.

It took me about sixty, but then I wasn't a crow.

It was really more like a house than a cabin. A pretty good-sized one with a wrap-around porch. It looked very out of place in the haunted woods because it was modern and the woods were not. The woods were old. There were four steps up to the porch.

I went up the stairs and knocked on the door. No one answered. I walked around the porch looking in windows without getting too close to them.

"Anyone home?" I shouted several times.

No one answered.

I went back to the front door and tried it. The door creaked open. I wondered if it was a requirement of all doors on the mountain that they creep.

"Anyone home?" I shouted again. On the third shout, I heard screaming.

It seemed someone was home, after all. The house was rustic, with a big living room and a kitchen off to the side. The living room had a fireplace that took up most of one wall.

I followed the screaming. In the kitchen, I found a door that opened up to a dark cellar. It had a pungent odor of sweaty socks and stagnate swamp water. I turned on the light. It didn't work. I didn't have my phone. I'd left it at the library. Now that I couldn't use it for calling or texting or the internet, it had lost most of its importance.

I should have brought it to the woods with me, though. I had to feel my way down the stairs. A railing would have helped. At the bottom, I found a light switch. A single dull lightbulb at the far end of the room flipped on. It was dull because it was red and the glow it gave off was tinted.

"What the fuck, man?" a boy said. "We've been screaming our heads off."

"Just get us out of here," a girl ordered.

"More lights?" I said to her.

"Get us out of here," another ordered.

They sounded feral. After my recent run in with Mrs. Johnson, the monster version, I was a little wary of voices in the dark. But these were just teenagers who, by nature, were monsters.

"I need more light," I said.

"There's a lamp over on the bench."

I went over to a workbench along the wall. I felt around and found it. I turned it on. This wasn't much better than the other, but at least it was clear and gave enough light to see. The room was small and crowded with torture devices and piles of old magazines and newspapers and a small sitting area with sofa, chairs and a TV. The teenagers were chained to the wall.

"Who are you anyway?" one girl said. She was pretty, blonde, skinny, with a pug nose.

"I'm the new librarian," I said. "Lady Blackstone asked me to come and find you. She was worried."

"Probably worried we ran off with Cousin Deadeye again."

"Another librarian?" Boy on the far end said. Tall and lanky. He looked older than the others, but probably wasn't.

"Barry was alive when we left," the other girl said. She had her mother's beauty except, in her case, the head was attached to the body. "Did you kill him?"

"Not me," I said.

"How?" she asked.

"Poison."

"Your father's good at poisons, isn't he?" A boy with

blonde hair said.

"He didn't poison him," the Blackstone girl said.

"Keys for the chains?" I said.

"Over there," the Blackstone girl said and nodded to her right.

I found a key ring hanging on a nail on a naked two-by-four.

"Torture chamber?" I asked.

"Love shack," the Blackstone girl said. "My mother likes to explore her sexuality. It's why she has to carry her head around with her."

"Makes sense," I said, looking around.

There were some medieval devices in the room. This was not the place for gentle experimentation. I unlocked the chains and let the teenagers free. They all rubbed their wrists, but other than that, they didn't seem hurt.

"So, your father's specialty is poisons?" I asked.

She glared at the boy who'd brought it up. The blonde boy smiled back. He had one of those smiles that was absolutely certain the world would smile back at him.

"So what?" she said. "There's plenty of others in town who know poisons. There's even Mrs. Morgan, who was hung for being a poisoner. I think she poisoned like a dozen old people."

We walked up the creaky stairs to the living room with its comfortable furniture and tall ceiling. A fire started in the fireplace when the Blackstone girl looked at it. Daughter of a magician and a witch. I suppose it was no surprise she had talents.

It had clouded up outside and was getting cooler. We sat in the furniture by the fireplace.

"Shouldn't she be dead?" I said. "Mrs. Morgan. If she was hung, I mean."

"It didn't take," the button nose girl said. "I'm Callie, by the way. Brandon's the one with the big mouth. The tall drink of water is Lonnie. Diana, the beautiful one."

"You don't have to say it like it's a crime," Diana said.

"Maybe it should be," Callie said.

"You can't hang someone twice,' Brandon said. "Did you know that?"

"I didn't," I said.

"Well, you can't if you're the state doing the hanging. I suppose you could if you were like some private individuals."

"I bet they kept hanging them until they got it done in the old West," Lonnie said. "They didn't like to leave a job undone."

Brandon got up and went over to the fire. He put his hands out and rubbed them together. "Mrs. Morgan didn't like the librarian. They were always fighting about something."

The room was heating up with the fire.

"Like what?"

"Everything. Her house is the closest one to the library. She said he was a bad neighbor. His nightmares drifted over to her house at night. That's what she told everyone."

"That does sound uncomfortable," I said.

"Are we staying another night?" Callie asked. "If we aren't, we'd better get going."

I understood the uneasy look on her face. None of us wanted to be caught in the woods at night.

"Let's go back," Diana said. "I hardly slept at all last night with Brandon's snoring."

"I don't snore," Brandon said. "I breathe heavily."

"Dude," Lonnie said. "You sound like a chainsaw."

Brandon shrugged. "At least I don't talk in my sleep."

They all looked at Diana.

"What did I say?" Diana said.

"Nothing," Callie said.

"Nothing. You just called Cousin Deadeye babe. The guy's what, like thousands of years old."

"Shut up," Callie said.

They all looked uneasy.

"Your mother said he kidnapped you," I said.

"We went with him," Diana said. "She just wants to make people think we were taken."

"Is he your boyfriend?" Lonnie said.

"It's none of your business," Diana said.

"You know what he is?"

"I don't," she said, "and you don't either."

"Fallen angel," I said. "One of Karl's agents is out to spread ruin among humans, including Supernaturals."

"What do you know?" Diana snapped.

"He's not on your side," I said. "He'll use anyone to get power or spread ruin. That's what he does."

"He's good to us," Diana said.

"How?" I asked.

"He doesn't lie to us. He told us about the people in town. What hypocrites they are."

"He says he'll get us out," Callie said.

"He'll get you off the mountain?" I said. "He says he can do that?"

"He did say that," Lonnie said. "If he's an angel, maybe he can."

"He's right about the adults," Brandon said. "My parents pretend like they're righteous believers in the gods and have these morals and everything, but my mom was screwing the librarian right along with all the other women in town."

"Not all," Callie said.

"Anyway," Brandon said. "Every adult told us there's no way off the mountain, but that's not true. He knows a way. And he's going to take us when he goes."

"They'll be a price," I said. "What's the price?"

They all looked away, and no one said a word.

"He might take you off," I said, "but find out where he'll take you to before you make your deal. It may not be where you want to go."

"How do you know all this about him?" Lonnie asked.

I told them about Vermont. I left out the part where he made it sound like Karl knew me and was protecting me and his insinuations. Karl was known for his trickery and his fallen angels and demons were known for the same. I couldn't trust anything they said. I'd made up my mind I wasn't going to let them influence me. I needed more information and proof before I would even consider that they were telling the truth.

When I'd told the teenagers about my run-in with Cousin Deadeye, they said nothing back. I could see they were all uneasy, even Diana. It made me more certain they didn't know what they were doing and Cousin Deadeye was going to use them for his own ends, maybe destroying them in the process.

"I want to go back to Eden now," Callie said.

I could have pressed on with what I thought I knew about Cousin Deadeye, but I didn't think any of them were ready to tell me what deal they'd struck with the black-winged angel. I'd wait for a better opportunity, maybe get Callie or possibly Lonnie alone. Anyway, the girl was right. We were running out of time.

We probably couldn't make it out of the haunted woods before the sun went down.

Chapter Nineteen

As we walked down the path, I told them I'd got lost on the way to find them. The woods were completely silent, which was a different kind of eerie than the chorus of birds or monkeys. There seemed to be numerous eerie in the haunted woods.

"It's easy to get lost in these woods," Diana said.

"It wouldn't be much of a haunted woods if people didn't get lost in it," Callie said.

I liked her sarcasm. She had, in my opinion, a good bad teenager attitude.

"I met the one-eyed witch of the woods," I said. "She sends her regards."

"You should have killed her," Brandon said.

"She wouldn't be easy to kill," Diana said. "She's powerful. Knows a lot of binding spells."

"Our parents would find her and they'd have a good old-fashioned witch burning if she'd hurt us," Brandon said. "She knew better."

"Why didn't she kill you?" Diana asked me.

"I have a sword," I said. I pulled it out of its sheath. It

sparkled even though there hadn't been any sunlight getting past the thick leaved branches of the tall trees a second ago. It was like it attracted light.

"Cool," Brandon said.

"Looks like a magic sword," Lonnie said.

"To be honest, I don't know how to use it but the witch didn't know that I didn't know."

"Our new librarian has some game," Brandon said.

The path became narrower than I remembered it. It was a rich part of the forest. I could smell the plants growing and the verdant black earth.

When we came to the clearing, I looked up at the tower. I had a feeling someone was watching us.

I gave them the finger.

The teenagers joined in. Not because they saw anyone or particularly cared that someone, likely Lord Blackstone, was watching, but because they didn't want to miss the chance to give someone the finger. Teenagers.

As we walked on, the quiet woods started to whisper. It reminded me of my first nights in the woods, lost and alone.

"I wish they'd just say what they want to say," Diana said.

I knew the power of whispers, though. Old magic.

"I think it's more a mood thing," Callie said. "Think horror films."

"Well, it's irritating," Diana said.

"Know any scary stories to tell in a haunted woods?" Brandon asked me.

"I know a lot of scary stories," I said.

"I wouldn't mind hearing one," Lonnie said. "These whispers get to me, too."

"They don't get to me," Diana said. "I just find them annoying."

"Whatever," Callie said. "Tell us a scary story, librarian."

"I know a lot of true ones from the road, but they are too scary. I'll tell you one I know from high school."

So, I did:

"When I was in high school, I got this call one night from a man who introduced himself as a Nightmare. I didn't want to talk to anyone with a name like that, so I hung up."

He called me back after a few minutes.

"I'm twenty miles away from you," he said. "I've been wanting to see you for the longest time. And now I'm coming."

"How did you know that? How did you know my family was gone?"

"I know a lot of things about you," the voice said.

I tried to place the voice, but I was sure I'd never heard it before. It was a man's voice, deeper than most, but otherwise not distinctive.

"Nineteen miles away," he said.

I hung up. I went to the front door and locked it, and I went to the back and made sure it was locked. I thought about calling my best friend Clementine, but she was dead. Also, dead was my friend Sammy. Both of them were killed by someone who called their phone numbers and said they were coming to visit. I knew this because they had both called the police.

I have to say, I was worried by these memories, and I jumped when the phone rang again.

"I'm fifteen miles away and I'm coming to see you," the voice said.

"What do you want?" I said.

"You know what I want."

"Not really," I said.

"Not really," he mocked.

I hung up. I thought about running out of the house and getting in my car and driving to the police station. Instead, I went down to the basement. Unfortunately, the lightbulb had recently burned out down there but at least my phone was still working and I could use the flashlight.

That was when I realized I was almost out of charge. I really needed to get better about charging my phone.

It rang again, but this time I had no intention of answering. I hit the decline. It kept ringing. I turned it off, which was troubling because the room went dark. The phone kept ringing.

I answered it.

"Stop calling" I said.

"Six miles away and I'm coming to see you."

"Just tell me what you want," I said.

"You know what I want."

"Stop saying that."

"You know what I want."

"I don't."

"Your friends said they didn't know either."

"Because maybe none of us know. Did you ever think of that? Did you ever think you're killing the wrong teenagers?"

"Let me think about," he said. "No, that's not it."

I should have been more prepared. I should have imagined this happening.

"Five miles away and I'm coming to see you," he said.

"And what are you going to do when you get here?"

"You know," he said.

I did kind of know. He'd eaten off the faces of my friends and pulled out all their guts. I thought he'd probably do the same to me.

"Eat my face and pull out all my guts?" I asked.

"Good guess."

"Four miles away and I'm coming to see you," he said.

I hung up. I remembered I had a dog. I ran upstairs, and the dog was in the kitchen. It was a small dog, though. It was not the kind of dog that was going to be much good against a murdering serial killer psychopath. She was called Cuddles.

I decided to hide back in the basement again. I let Cuddles come with me. The flashlight went out as we were going down the stairs. I tripped over Cuddles and ended up on the floor.

My phone rang. It was dead, but it rang.

"I'm turning down your block now. I'm driving down your street."

I tried to hang up, but since I'd never answered and the phone was dead, hanging up didn't do any good.

"I'm pulling up your drive."

I could hear my breathing it was so hard.

"I'm walking up to your front door."

It banged open.

"Come out, come out, wherever you are," he said in a singsong voice.

Cuddles started to bark. I told her no, but she just kept on. That dog never listened to anybody.

The basement door swung open.

The End.

* * *

"Not bad, librarian," Brandon said.

Then they wanted to know some real stories, especially after I told them I'd been on the road for years before I ended up in Eden.

"Too scary," I reminded them.

When we were almost back in town, Callie asked me if I had ever met an angel in my travels. I said that I had met a couple. One black winged, who we'd already talked about. Another white winged.

"Why?" I asked.

"My mother claims my father was an angel. Since you're the librarian and all, I thought maybe you could help me find out which one."

"You think the answer is in the library?"

"My mother's story is that the angel came to her in the night and they had sex and I was born three days later."

"It was someone married in town," Diana said. "you know that. She's just trying to hide his identity from you."

"I don't know anything for sure. That's why I'm asking the librarian."

"Shouldn't you have wings or something if you've got angel blood?" Brandon asked.

"Should I?" Callie asked me.

I said I didn't know.

She looked sad, so I said I would do a little research and see if I could find out anything. I was a sucker for sad looks.

Chapter Twenty

After the teenagers and I got back from the cabin, I went to the library. I made a cup of coffee and put the sword back in the curiosities collection. Then I went upstairs and did a walk around the library and drank my coffee. The upstairs rooms were buzzing when I came in. Some of the magic books were putting up a fuss. And Dr. Jekyll and Mr. Hyde had slipped out of their novel and were arguing, their ghostly appearances inches away from each other over by the window. Mr. Hyde was jamming his finger into what would have been Dr. Jekyll's chest if he had a chest.

"I demand my own book. I am by far the more interesting," Mr. Hyde said.

Like all dynamic fictional characters, they seemed to jump right off the page, only in this case they had actually jumped right off the page.

"I created you," Dr. Jekyll said. "And I can destroy you."

"I will burn this library to the ground, and then I will dance on its ashes," Mr. Hyde screamed, and he took a punch at Dr. Jekyll. Fortunately, since he had no substance, the punch went right through him. This seemed to infuriate Dr. Jekyll, who counter punched with a roundhouse so round he landed on the floor.

I found a spell book in the magic room and looked through it and found a calming spell a librarian had created not long after acquiring the Robert Louis Stevens's novel. The magic book said you did not have to be a magician or witch or wizard to do a spell. You just needed to say the right words the right way. That was something I knew how to do from hypnotism, something I had practiced many times and struggled to improve.

I failed three times, but the fourth time the spell calmed Dr. Jekyll and Mr. Hyde enough that I could force them back into the book whose title bore their names.

I looked in a room devoted to books on supernatural beings. I asked for a book on angels who had visited Eden and one flew off the shelves and into my hands. It had been written by a former librarian, one who had, according to the biography written by another librarian, been the librarian from 2017 to 2018.

There was a section in a document titled, strangely enough, Angel Visitations. Apparently, there had been dozens of angel visitations over the past five hundred years, which, apparently, was when the librarians started documenting some aspects of the library. But there were no dates and only brief descriptions of visiting angels.

The angel Michael showed up today. He was in a foul mood, itching for a fight. He went down the mountain to see if he could find any demons to tangle with. He found Cousin Deadeye, a demon of some repute, who lived on the other side of the mountain. Some say he is one of the fallen angels, which no doubt would have worsened Michael's mood.

The Librarian of The Haunted Library

They got into a fight that lasted for six days. On the seventh, they had dinner together. It was said by some that if an archdemon and an archangel could have dinner together, perhaps there was hope for the future.

What had happened to that hope? Had it ever really existed?

One of the more recent angels to visit was Gabriel, the angel of mysteries. There was a veiled reference to his secret visits to one in Eden who he held in esteem above all others. This sounded like a promising candidate.

The library bell rang. I went to the door. Today it had blue glass. I could see two people out on the front step but not clear through the color blue. I opened the door.

"Good evening," I said. "Come in."

"No thanks," Ryan said. "Just on our way over to the bar."

"We stopped by to ask you to come and have a drink with us," Camila said. "We heard you went out to the woods. If you're going to do things like that, we thought we better have a drink before we miss our window of opportunity."

"Don't say that, Camila," Ryan said. Then he looked at me. "But it's true. You're pushing the envelope."

"It wasn't that bad," I said, though I suppose if I hadn't had the magic sword I would be dead. I made a mental note to thank Olive.

"It's been a long day," I said.

"On us," Ryan said. "Come on. A quick one."

"All right. Let me just turn off the computer."

I went back to my desk and got out of the library files and closed the computer with its protected password that was actually Password so, yeah, not protected. But who could get into the library besides one very sneaky ghoul?

Anyway, demons were notoriously bad with computers. Something in their DNA. I suppose it was a stereotype, but I'd never met a demon who could interact with machines well. On the other hand, that didn't mean there wasn't one. I changed the password to Dr. Jekyll and Mr. Hyde, which was at least one rung up from Password.

We went to the bar and sat in one of the booths. Ryan said he would go get the drinks.

"Beer for me."

"How about an Eden Garden of Delight?"

"Sure," I said.

When he walked away, I asked Camila if she knew Angela Morgan.

"The poisoner? I know her to say hello. It's a small town. I know most people enough to say hello."

"One of the teenagers told me she'd been hung."

"Didn't take," Camila said.

"She poisoned old people? That's what they said."

"The teenagers mention she was a nurse?"

"They didn't," I said.

"Killed terminal patients. No one thinks she was doing it for fun. She poisoned them in a humanitarian way."

"The jury must have thought she murdered them," I said.

"When I was a girl, we had a dog that got very sick. We put the dog to sleep because we loved him so much. It was a kindness. We hoped there was a better place on the other side. But we knew how terrible the pain he was in was. We saw it. And we helped him. I don't think it was wrong."

"You've got a point. What I'm trying to get to, though, is she had the skills to poison the librarian. Now I wonder if she had a motive. The teenagers say she did. The two argued and maybe she decided to turn to an old method to solve her problem with the librarian."

"There are others who know poisons in this town. I'm very good at poisons."

"Did you kill the librarian?"

"No," she said. "But I guess you're asking cause you know he and I were more than just friends and a whole lot less too. I did have an affair with him. Please don't tell Ryan. There was just something about the man that was hard to resist."

"He was handsome," I said.

"That wasn't it," she said.

"A powerful magician. A powerful man who knew things, secrets."

"Yes," she said.

"What else?"

"Other women were attracted to him. For some, it was a competition."

"He was a practicer of the dark arts, wasn't he?"

This was a guess, but I had learned enough about him to make it.

"Yes," she said. "He was a powerful dark arts magician. A lot of women were drawn to him."

"What about Lord Blackstone?"

"What about him?"

"Were they friends? Enemies? Frenemies?"

"I suppose I'd say they were allies. You think Lord Blackstone killed him?"

"Not anymore," I said.

Ryan came back with two beers and a whiskey, neat. That was for Camila. He sat next to her.

"What have you two been talking about?" he asked.

"Murder," I said.

"Who we going to kill?" he said.

"In the past," I said.

"Ah," he said. "There's a pool, you know. I was just talking to the bartender about it. Ninety percent of the participants think you'll be gone in a week."

"I heard," I said. "When you say gone, do you mean moved on to another town?"

"Ah, no," he said.

I took a sip of my beer. It was a great beer. It tasted like the beer commercials promised, like something that could change your life. Almost.

"This tastes great."

"Everything tastes better up here. It's one benefit of living on a mountain."

"Not usually a benefit," I pointed out.

"No," Camila said. "In case you haven't noticed, there's a lot of not usually here."

"Actually, I have," I said. "Can you tell me why?"

She shook her head. "Don't know. No one does or if they do, they aren't telling."

"Why are we born? Why do we die? Why do we dream?" Ryan said. "You want to talk about weird shit? It's all pretty weird."

I thought Ryan might have more to him that I'd originally thought. I had come to the opinion that most people did. One way or another.

"My boy has a point," Camila said. "The world is a strange place."

"What did I miss?" Ryan said. "You two looked like you were having an intense conversation while I was at the bar."

"We were talking about the former librarian," I said. "Seems he was quite the ladies' man."

The Librarian of The Haunted Library

"He was the kind liked to talk about it. Brag. Some of the women were married. It was bound to end in trouble. It's a small town. A librarian has a target on his back, anyway. But he was very powerful, very aware. I'm surprised someone was able to poison him."

"Maybe because it was an expert doing the poisoning"

"There's a disturbingly high number of experts here in Eden," Ryan said.

Camila had become quiet. She downed her whiskey in one smooth movement.

"Are you all right?" he said, finally noticing her silence.

"Headache," she said.

"Want to head out?"

"I think I'll go home. You stay."

She said good night and left. Ryan walked her out. When he came back, he said, "Let me tell you about my adoption from the orphanage."

He told me, in detail. I smiled in the right places. I congratulated him.

"I was lucky," he said.

"You were," I agreed.

It was dark outside the windows. I guess it had been dark for some time.

"You know what time it is?"

"Close to midnight, I guess."

Time worked strangely on the mountain. It seemed to speed up and slow down, which was impossible.

We left after we finished our beers. He wanted to get home to check on Camila.

As I walked back to the library, I wondered why Olive lied to me about not hooking up with the librarian? She wasn't married. The librarian wasn't married. So, she had an affair. So what. Maybe she was just embarrassed because he'd seduced her. But I couldn't overlook the obvious. She had opportunity. Easy to add a little something to the tea. Did she have motive?

I hoped not.

Chapter Twenty-One

I woke up to the boom of thunder and the flash of lightning. I was in the basement so all I had were little windows near the ceiling, but the flashes were big ones and for a second lit up the room.

The woman in the red dress standing in the corner gave me quite a start. I jumped up out of bed. Then I recognized her. She was an old teacher of mine from the sixth grade. She had been the most beautiful teacher I'd ever had. All the boys who had just started having boners had had boners for her. I saw her in a flash of lightning. I also saw she was holding something behind her back.

"Ms. Thompson?" I said.

She sure looked like Ms. Thompson.

"I'm finally going to make your dream come true," she said.

She sounded like Ms. Thompson, but the words were not her words. She would never say *make your dream come true*.

"Come over here, Ms. Thompson," I said.

Another flash of lightning. She moved quickly across

the floor. Her feet didn't appear to touch, which was likely the reason her speed seemed effortless. The smile was a little off, but physically, otherwise, everything else was just as I remembered it. Except the moving across the floor without taking steps, of course.

"I'm going to give you a happy ending," she said.

"Take off your clothes, Ms. Thompson," I said.

"I like the way you think. You young boys are so frisky."

The lightning flashed over the room, and I saw she had taken off her clothes. She was one quick undresser. She still had one hand behind her back.

"What's that you have behind your back?" I asked.

"A love toy for your pleasure," she said.

Next flash of lightening her hand wasn't behind her back anymore. She had lied. She had something in her hand. It was a hatchet.

"You brought me a present," I said.

I could feel my heart beating very hard, and it wasn't because of her naked body. At least most of it wasn't because of her naked body. The erection, however, was because of her naked body. Well, she had always been a favorite teacher of mine.

She was right next to me, so close I could feel her breath. There was another flash of lightning. I saw her arm raising and the ax glint in the light. Someone had put a nice polish on its blade.

I just hoped the chapter on ghouls I'd read was accurate. The source had been questionable because it was a monk who seemed to believe that the way to true religious knowledge was meditation after eating a meal of psychedelic mushrooms.

Before Ms. Thompson could bring the axe down on my head and split it like kindling for a fire, I puckered up and moved in. I suckled her breast. I suckled it for all I was worth, knowing that if this didn't work, that ax was going to split me in two.

"No," she cried.

She dropped the axe. She still looked like Ms. Thompson. I kept suckling her breast, just to be sure. The chapter in the book by the monk had said if a human suckles a female ghoul's breast, she is obliged to serve him.

"I would like you to stop trying to kill me," I said when I took my mouth off her nipple.

She stepped back and looked at me with disdain. "Fine."

"I can't believe that worked," I said.

"That's the problem these days," the ghoul said. "Everybody knows things they shouldn't know. In the old days, no one ever suckled my breast. No one had a clue. Now it's not just librarians who know. I blame the internet."

I knew better than to let a demon get talking about their grievances. They could go on forever.

"Anyway," I said. "Why are you here to kill me?"

"Orders," she said.

"Karl?"

"Karl? No."

"So not Karl. A fallen angel then or a demon? A jealous one or a worried one or a devious one? Maybe Cousin Deadeye?"

"Stop making wild guesses."

"I don't think I have any other kind in this case."

"Wrong side," she said.

"Wait. Really?"

"Really."

"Who?" I asked.

"I can't tell you. Just so you know, it's someone important."

"But Christian mythos? Not Greek or Buddhist or Navajo or Star Wars or any of the others."

"Christian."

"It's God?"

She looked disgusted. "Of course, it's not God. He doesn't order hits."

"A white-winged angel?" I said.

"Finally. Never go on Jeopardy. You will embarrass yourself out of your shoes."

"That's not a saying."

"It was in Babylon. It just doesn't translate well."

"Why?"

"It's an ancient language. Some things don't."

"I meant why would an angel from heaven want me dead?"

"I don't have to tell you. I won't kill you since you suckled my breast, but angels have rights, too. More importantly, the angel in question has power over me. I couldn't tell you even if I wanted to. And I don't. Not bad suckling, though."

"Thank you."

"Would you like to see what you really suckled?"

"No," I said. "How'd you get into the library?"

"I don't have to tell you."

"I'm not getting as much out of my suckling as I hoped," I said.

"Life is full of disappointments."

"Forgive me, but you seem like you would work for Karl. I'm not sure I believe you about the angel."

"You humans overestimate Karl and, at the same time, underestimate him. Karl doesn't know all that much, but he knows one thing that gets you humans every time. He knows you all have secret yearnings and secrets you don't want told."

"That's two things," I said.

"They're related. 1A and 1B."

"Which is two things."

"Anyway," she said. "He helps you achieve your yearning, or he helps you hide your secret. That's not so innovative, but he gets a lot of credit."

"You sound jealous."

"I give him props for his rebellion against the big guy, but he did lose, after all."

"I don't know," I said. "Still sounds like sour grapes."

"I'm just a working girl," she said. "I kill for whoever hires me. Angel. Demon. Makes no difference. But it's not Karl."

"Leave the library now, please," I said.

"You asking?"

"Order," I said. "Leave the library."

She disappeared.

The lightning and thunder stopped.

I had a restless night. I'd come to believe the messages I got from the cosmos were from a force for good. I even sometimes thought they were from an angel or even god himself. Now an angel was trying to kill me? Why?

Chapter Twenty-Two

The next morning, I went to see the mayor before my library shift started. He was in his office. His secretary wasn't in yet, but the door was open. The mayor was sitting at his desk. He had a cup of coffee in his hand. He was staring out the window. He had a nice window to stare out of. He could see the whole square.

"Librarian," he said. "You're up early."

"I had a restless night."

"Those come wherever you are. Even if you're dead. The term rolling over in your grave is not just metaphorical."

"I don't think we're dead," I said.

"Everyone is entitled to their opinion. Pour yourself a cup of coffee and sit down."

I went over to the coffeepot and I noticed a painting on the wall that hadn't been there before. It was of the mayor as a young man. He seemed to be shaking the hand of someone who looked suspiciously like Abraham Lincoln.

I added cream and three sugars to my coffee because,

especially when I had my first cup, I liked my coffee sweet. I went back over and sat down across from the mayor.

"That looks like Abraham Lincoln in the picture," I said.

"Very astute."

The mayor had a little snark in him. I'd noticed this before.

"You shook Abraham Lincoln's hand?"

"I've been hearing good things about you," he said. "I am pleased I chose you as librarian."

"What good things?" I said.

"You met the one-eyed witch of the woods and survived. You rescued our teenagers. That witch has been pushing the evil envelope for years. Excellent job. You will be a good librarian."

"So, you aren't betting in the pool about how long I'll last, then?"

"There's a pool?" he said.

Not very convincing. I was surprised. He was a politician.

"So, you are betting?"

He shrugged.

"Death or running away?" I said.

"Well," he said. "No time to talk about that right now. I've got work to get back to."

"Sure," I said.

If staring out the window is your work—I didn't say.

"What's on your mind?" he asked.

"The last librarian being poisoned is on my mind a lot."

"Poison is the most common killer of librarians. Be careful what you eat. Most unique was the time a librarian was run over by a car."

"I didn't think there were any cars here," I said.

He nodded sagely. "Exactly."

"But," I said, "how could someone be run over by a car if there are no cars in Eden?"

"It's a head scratcher for sure. Now, son, I'm a busy man. I can only give you another minute or two."

"Who was the librarian's best friend?" I said.

"He didn't really have any friends."

"None?" I said. "What about you?"

"We weren't really friends. More like colleagues."

"No friends?"

"No friends that were just friends," the mayor said.

"What were they then?"

"Friends with benefits. And they never lasted very long. To be perfectly honest, he was a rake, a player, a ladies' man."

"He loved women?" I said.

"You could say that."

"Would you say that? You were his best friend. People have told me."

"We had drinks occasionally. We worked together from time to time. No more."

"You said he wasn't a great librarian. Not the worst. Not the best. Why? I've heard he was a powerful magician."

"That's true. He had great potential. He just couldn't focus on his job."

"What's that mean?"

He took a sip of his coffee. "I won't speak ill of the dead. They don't like it. Sometimes it wakes them up. You don't want that. A grumpy librarian angry about being awakened isn't good for anyone."

"You said he wasn't the best, and he wasn't the worst librarian. The first night I was here, you said that."

The Librarian of The Haunted Library

"He couldn't stay focused on the job. He had too many things going on in his life. You'll see."

"What will I see?" I asked.

"The librarian has responsibilities that aren't apparent at first. He did not always live up to those responsibilities. That's all I'll say about that."

"He was involved with a lot of women. That was one of the distractions?" I said.

"Absolutely."

"Some women he was involved with were married?"

"Some," he said.

"Could be he was murdered by a jealous husband?"

"Could be," he said.

I finished my coffee. It was already cold. It felt a little cool in the mayor's office. I thought the temperature had dropped. I looked around with my third eye and was relieved not to see the librarian's ghost.

"You didn't kill him, did you?" I asked the mayor.

"Of course not."

"You were friends. Sometimes friends kill each other."

"Why would I kill him?" He threw up his arms as if to illustrate physically the absurdity of my question.

"Why would you?" I said.

"I asked you first."

"Why would you?"

"Quit saying that," he said.

I sat back. The mayor wore nice suits.

"How many women do you think he had affairs with?"

"Depends what you mean by affairs."

"More than sleeping with them one night, let's say."

"No idea," he said.

"Dozens?"

"Sure, probably dozens."

"Are you married, mayor?"

"Widower," he said.

"Involved with anyone."

"Not that it's any of your business, but yes, I am. Charlotte Harris and I are dating."

"Did the librarian ever date her?"

"For heaven's sake. No. Not attractive enough for him."

"But the librarian dated dozens of women. Slept with them."

"No law against that. He was young and attractive and available. The women were willing. We're all adults here. Well, except for the four teenagers."

"Did he give them gifts? These women."

"Barry? No. They gave Barry gifts. He'd brag about it."

"What gifts?"

"Clothes. Some property, I believe. He was going to build a house, have one built. Now let me ask you a question."

"Sure."

"The clown," he said. "You said he kicked you out of his car."

"That's right."

"Was he wearing the clown's feet?"

"He was."

"That must have hurt."

"The landing hurt."

"No doubt," he said. "Look, Kevin, the former librarian was no saint. He didn't do anything illegal. He was not a great person to get involved with, but what's that they say? All's fair in love and war."

Something about the former librarian was elusive. I was missing something.

"Thank you for your time, Mayor," I said, standing.

"Be safe," he said.

Then I had another thought.

"Is there someone in town who knows everyone's business?"

"You mean like a fortuneteller?"

"I was thinking the town gossip," I said.

"Sonya Wishbone is the oldest woman in town. She lives in the pink house at the end of Main Street. She's a fortune teller. Might be helpful. Sometimes we use her to help us with the annual budget."

The houses didn't have addresses. Pink house at the end of the street or that house that has the statue of a mule out in front—was what they had instead of street numbers.

"She helps you see the future so you can balance the budget?" I said.

"What?"

"Fortuneteller."

"Don't be ridiculous. She was an accountant when she lived in San Diego. Years ago. Probably over a hundred. Her house is the oldest house in town."

"That makes sense," I said.

He frowned. "Why?"

"She's the oldest woman."

"I suppose you librarians think differently than the rest of us," he said in a distinctly disapproving voice. "I'd better get back to work."

He didn't have papers on his desk or a computer open. He leaned back in his chair and closed his eyes.

"What work are you doing?" I asked.

He opened his eyes. "Are you still here?"

"I'm leaving," I said.

"See you this evening," he said.

"All right," I said. "Wait, why this evening?"

"Didn't you hear the announcement yesterday from Marta?"

"I was probably off in the woods."

"I'd stay out of the woods if I were you. Or at least stay out of them for three weeks."

"Because you've got three weeks in the pool?"

"Not necessarily," he said.

"But you do."

He shrugged. "I'm saving up for a vacation."

I was about to ask him where he would go on vacation, but realized I might never get out of that office if I didn't stick to the topic.

"The announcement?" I said. "What did it say?"

"Town meeting tonight."

"Where?"

"In the town square. If you could say a few words, that would be excellent. Put people's mind at ease. You are supposed to be their protector, after all. Some think you're not doing a great job. Already one librarian has died since you've come to town."

"I wasn't even the librarian then."

"Now is not the time to quibble. Just reassure them."

"I'm not much of a public speaker." As in, not at all. As in, I didn't even like crowds.

"Just so they can see your face. And tell them your qualifications. Make yourself seem like the kind of person who does not wander into town from the woods and takes over."

"All right," I said reluctantly

"And get in something about you being the right man for the job."

"I don't really have any qualifications."

"Don't be silly," he said. "You're one of the most qualified candidates we've ever had. There was a Witcher once who passed through. He might have been more qualified, but he wouldn't take the job. Couldn't give up the life of a drifter. Anyway, you go along now. See you tonight."

Fighting monsters was one thing, but public speaking, that was really scary.

Chapter Twenty-Three

I went to Sonya Wishbone's house at the end of Main Street. Last house on the left and only pink house in town. I went up to the door and pressed the doorbell. About five minutes later, the door opened, and a woman stood there. I remembered her from my first night in town. She was in the café when my predecessor died. She used a walker that had tennis balls on the front two legs.

"Librarian," she said. "I've been expecting you."

"Really?" I said, surprised.

"Sorry it took me so long to come to the door. I was back praying in the laundry room."

I nodded as if to say, *No problem. Been there many times. Hard to hear the doorbell when you're praying in the laundry room and have the washer and dryer going.* But I said nothing.

"Come in, librarian."

I followed her in. We made our way to the living room, which was only about ten feet away. But because she took tiny steps, it took several minutes. She had coffee out on a tray and two cups. I realized she'd literally been expecting me.

"How'd you know I was coming?"

"I know things," she said. "Also, the mayor called me."

"You have a phone?" I said. I'd only seen one other in town and that was in Lucy's.

"No," she said. "There's milk and sugar for your coffee. You prefer milk over cream if I'm not mistaken."

"You're not but how—"

I noticed on an end table that there was a crystal ball and something that looked like large cards wrapped in red satin. We sat on the sofa and I made my coffee the way I liked it. The coffee was better than the mayor's.

"I just had a few questions."

"You have many questions. You're a questioner. That's all right. The world needs questioners."

"The mayor called the librarian a player."

"Did he?"

"He seems to have a lot of relationships."

"We were clear with each other from the start. No long-term."

"You didn't want a long-term relationship with him?"

"In my condition? I'm not interested in a long-term anything."

"What's your condition?"

"I'm old."

"This was a sexual relationship?"

"I'm old," she said, "not dead. We got it on like we used to back in the sixties. Love the one you're with and all that."

I wasn't sure what she was talking about, but I got the gist of it.

"Was he involved with someone else when he was with you?"

"He was an excellent lover. Word got around."

"So he was."

"I thought he might be involved with the blacksmith, but that went south when they got into an argument over whether horse shoes were lucky."

"I didn't realize there were horses in town," I said.

"There aren't," she said.

I took another sip of my coffee.

"Was he kind?"

"Seldom," she said. "And he wasn't honest either. Some did say he was a bad-breaker upper, but I was fine with how things ended between us."

"How did they end?"

"Abruptly, but on friendly terms."

"But you heard he was a bad breaker upper."

"That's the rumor."

"You heard it from more than one source, didn't you?"

She took a drink of her coffee. She raised her pinky. I'd never seen anyone raise their pinky before. Maybe I was in the presence of royalty. But why the pinky? Some rules of etiquette seemed pretty random to me. Like a bunch of rich, powerful people got together on Sunday afternoon at the club and came up with crazy shit to make people do.

"I did," she said.

"Was he violent with any of the women?"

"To the best of my knowledge, no. I think he wasn't averse to rough sex, and some of the women in town enjoy it. But as far as physical abuse, no."

She walked me to the door, her baby steps making it a slow go. I asked her, because it had been bothering me, "Why do you pray in the laundry room?"

"That's where the god is."

I nodded. But then realized I was doing it again—

nodding at something I didn't understand. I'd been doing that a lot since I came to Eden.

"Seems a strange place for a god to hang out."

"I suppose so," she said, "in most cases. But not this one."

We came to the door. I opened it.

"You see, he's a minor god," she said.

"Lots of those around," I said.

"The god of the lost socks."

"Ah," I said. "Makes sense."

"Yes," she nodded.

I stepped outside.

"But," I said. "Isn't praying to a god who takes one of your socks sort of counterproductive?"

"Yes, but it's a wonder, isn't it?" she said. "Where does the sock go?"

"I suppose it is," I said.

"I'm praying to him because he gives me a sense of wonder and it only costs me one sock."

She shut the door. I walked down the sidewalk. As deals with gods went, I had to admit it was a pretty good one.

Chapter Twenty-Four

I opened the library at nine. The government worker, named Mr. Rosenbottom, was in a bad mood.

"This place does not feel as organized as when former librarians were running it. You are not a neat person. Look at your own appearance."

I was wearing my jeans, a t-shirt, and tennis shoes.

"It's what I wear," I said, though I varied it some. Boots instead of tennis shoes. Occasionally an untucked button shirt.

"My point exactly. You know, the last librarian always wore nice suits. He had his faults, but he was neat. A civil servant should always be neat in appearance and in performing his duties."

"Nice to see you, Mr. Rosenbottom."

I guess it was a little dismissive, but I felt like being a little dismissive. Sometimes it was necessary to keep up the spirits.

He frowned and abruptly turned away and walked over to get the newspaper.

The teenager, Callie, came into the library after a few

minutes and wanted to know if I had learned anything about her father. I told her I had a good prospect. An angel named Gabriel had made several visits to the town over the years. He was said to be visiting someone he held in esteem.

"That's all it said. And there aren't any dates, so I can't be sure when this was, but he's a possibility."

"Do I look like him?"

"There wasn't a picture," I said. "Why don't you just ask your mother?"

"She won't tell me anything. She says that it's for my own good."

Callie asked me to find any books we had that mentioned Gabriel, and I went up to the second floor. The books were talking, but they stopped suddenly when I came into the room, which made me suspicious they'd been talking about me. Maybe I was just being paranoid.

"Anyone who has anything on Gabriel the Angel, please come to me."

According to the librarian manual, this was how the librarian found books he wanted. A polite call was all that was needed.

There were some noises. Several books said they had one sentence, and I changed the search to ask for a minimum of one paragraph on Gabriel the Angel.

Three books came to me. I took them downstairs to Callie, who was sitting in one of the chairs by a window. She was reading something from a book she'd found on the shelves.

"Thanks," she said.

"I can help you," I said. "If Cousin Deadeye has you caught up in something and you don't know how to get out, I can help."

"He doesn't," she said. "He understands how messed up this town is."

"Messed up how?"

"They treat us like we don't belong here because we were left on the church stairs. We were babies. Then my mother starts telling everyone she's my real mother and my father is an angel. So, then they think we're crazy. Only then do the other parents admit that the baby they adopted is their baby, too."

"I don't understand," I said.

"No one understands. Four women had babies without being pregnant for more than a few days, and all four were told to place their babies on the church steps by some mysterious force. They did, but they adopted us after one night. I guess it's not a big surprise the town has always been suspicious of us. It still hurts."

"And no one knows how any of this happened?"

"No kids born here before or since," she said. "It's freaking weird, right? But it's not our fault."

"No," I said. "It's not."

"And all of you have seen the world off the mountain. We're the only four that haven't seen it at all. But our parents won't even try to get us off. They say it's too dangerous. Cousin Deadeye understands that."

"And uses it," I said. "Anyway, your father could be an angel."

"Gabriel," she said.

"He could be," I said.

"You know he talked about you."

"Who?"

"Cousin Deadeye. He said you might come. There was a prophecy that you would return to Eden. He said you were an orphan and you would destroy our town."

"He can't be trusted."

"He also said that you know who your father is but won't admit it."

"I know who he wants me to think my father is."

"Who?"

"Karl."

"But you don't believe it?"

"Honestly, I don't know. I'm going to need more proof before I accept he's my father."

She went over to the living room to read. Rosenbottom frowned at her. He obviously disapproved of the young on principle, but then he seemed to disapprove of every age. He might be an equal opportunity disapprover.

I stepped out of the library onto the front porch. I wished I had a healthy cigarette. I wondered if anyone would even want to smoke a healthy cigarette if someone invented one. I thought I would. But was the fact that cigarettes were unhealthy for you, deadly possibly, an essential part of smoking's charm? I thought I remembered Kurt Vonnegut writing that smoking was a slow form of suicide. Could be an important part of enjoying a smoke was the rebellion not only against social norms but against life itself.

Eden was warming up. The nights were cold on the mountain, but the days, so far, mostly warm.

Callie had said that Cousin Deadeye said some prophecy predicted I would return to Eden. What prophecy? I went back to the library and looked up books on prophecy about the son of Karl. There were many of them, mostly having to do with the destruction of the world and the end of humankind.

I didn't want to be the Prince of Darkness. I certainly didn't want to be the announcement of The End of Days, which would lead up to the final battle between the Kingdom of Heaven and the Kingdom of Hell.

I closed up the library at eleven, hungry because I hadn't eaten any breakfast.

Right after I closed up, the ghost appeared.

"Were you a pilot of a riverboat?" I said before he could say anything.

"You think I'm Mark Twain?" he said. "Don't be ridiculous. I'm much better looking than that old codger."

"You knew him?"

"I knew him. We were friends though I'll tell you truly, it wasn't always easy. The most foolish man with money I ever met. But he had wit. I had to give him that. And he knew language. He once said, the difference between the right word and the almost right word is the difference between the lightning and the lightning bug."

"That's a good one," I said.

"I have bad news," the ghost said.

"What's the bad news?"

"That demon that you banished is still here."

"I thought so," I said. "She went a little too easy for a demon assassin. A ghoul assassin, as it turns out."

"Is that what she is? A ghoul. Yes. I see it. Ghouls are known for their vanity. She might be getting serious about you."

"If she's looking for a long-term relationship, I'm a bad bet," I said.

"I meant in killing you. No more fooling about with costume bodies from your past. Better watch yourself."

"I'm touched by your warning."

"I need you to get me out. You'll have a better chance if you're alive."

He disappeared.

Chapter Twenty-Five

I was walking over to the café when I saw the teenagers in the park. I went over to them. They were sitting in a circle on the grass.

"Mr. Librarian," Brandon said. "What's up dude?"

He was stoned. Looked like the girls were, too. Hard to tell about Lonnie.

"Was there any woman in town that the librarian wasn't sleeping with?" I asked them.

Brandon laughed. "The man was a sex machine."

"Shut up," Diana said.

"Just the truth."

"There were some," Lonnie said.

"I never slept with him," Callie said.

"But not all of us teenagers can say that, can we?" Brandon said.

"Shut up," Diana said.

"You sure tell people to shut up a lot," I said.

Callie said, giggling. "He's right. You do."

"It's just better if we don't talk about it with this librarian," Diana said. "He's just trying to get us to tell him things. Why should we? Anyway, we were warned."

"If you know who killed my predecessor, then, yes, I'd like you to tell me. But I don't think you do. You do know something, though."

"What do we know?" Lonnie said.

"Did Cousin Deadeye tell you to kill the librarian?"

"No," Brandon said.

"We didn't kill him," Lonnie said. "You just said so yourself."

"He just told us to take care of our parents," Diana said. She had thick long hair, and she pushed it out of her eyes, maybe a little more often than was absolutely necessary. "That's all. Take care of them."

"That's not all," Lonnie said.

"My father is an angel," Callie said. She looked at the others as if daring them to argue. "The librarian told me."

"Whatever," Diana said.

"We weren't supposed to kill him," Lonnie said. "We were supposed to keep him from being killed."

"But you left town?" I said.

They looked at each other.

"He was supposed to come with us," Callie said.

"He didn't show," Brandon said.

"Cousin Deadeye wanted to meet him?" I guessed.

"Yes," Diana said. "But he wasn't going to kill him, if that's what you're thinking. He thought Barry could serve him."

"How?"

"We don't know," Callie said.

"You don't even know him," Diana said, glaring at me and pushing her hair back with her hand. "You act like he's a monster but you don't even know him."

"I saw him turn a nice little town into one where everyone was trying to harm one another, even kill one another. He did what he set out to do. He turned brothers against brothers and friends against friends. He created hate. That's what Cousin Deadeye does. It's his vocation."

"The world has dark and light," Diana said. "My father always says that. Someone has to be the dark. My family is willing to be what others are afraid to be. What you're afraid to be."

"You mean you have a natural inclination," I said. "Maybe I do too, but I choose not to give into it. A lot of evil is just selfishness."

They all looked uneasy. I was uneasy. People thought they were born in the light or in the dark. But everyone had some of both. The amounts were the difference. What you did with those amounts were the difference.

"I've got to get home," Diana said.

The others went with her.

This town on this mountain in this dark wood was not here by accident. It had some purpose in what was to come and in what had been. I saw that in a flash with my third eye. Winged men and women, angels, with white wings fighting those with black wings in aerial combat.

And then another moment from long ago. A man and a woman naked in the garden, and the man saying, "Look, you're taller, that's why. You can reach it. Just get up on your tippy toes and pluck it from the tree. You think He can see everything just because He told us He could see everything? Of course, he'd say that. He's just trying to scare us. Go on, pluck it. I want to taste something sweet."

She reached out.

And history was made.

Chapter Twenty-Six

I went over to the café. I joined the lunch rush and had to sit at the counter because all the tables and booths were taken. Olive was working. She worked the breakfast-lunch shifts four days a week and the lunch-dinner shifts two days. Seemed like a lot of shifts to me, but she said she was saving up for a goat.

"Find the killer yet?" Olive asked as she brought me coffee.

"Not yet," I said. "Three steps forward and two back, or maybe two steps forward and three back. I'm not sure."

She asked me what I wanted. I went with the meatloaf special.

Rip Van Winkle sat down next to me. He said he was very disappointed in me. Turned out he'd thought I'd only last a day and here it was day two.

"I'm disappointed in you," I said. "One day? You must not have thought much of me."

"I just know some things."

"Like what?"

"I could tell you if you buy me lunch."

The Librarian of The Haunted Library

"Lunch?"

"Just a cheeseburger and fries. I left my wallet at home."

"Does anyone ever believe you when you say that?"

"Sure. People who don't know me."

"Fine," I said. "Lunch."

"The previous librarian came from California. He was hiking in that Sequoia forest out there. You ever been? Those trees are something to see. I myself have been around the world two times. There's so many things to see out there; I don't understand how people can spend their whole life in one place."

"I've seen the forest of giant redwoods north of San Francisco," I said. "How did you get here?"

Olive came, and he ordered his cheeseburger and fries.

"On his bill," he said, nodding at me. "And make it rare. I want it to bleed."

I told her to put it on my bill. She shook her head as if I was being foolish, probably because I was being foolish.

"I came from the Everglades. My best friend dumped me out there because he was in love with my wife. Can you imagine that? He shot me first and left me to be eaten by alligators. But I beat the odds."

"Did you?" I said.

"You aren't joining Deadheads, are you?" he said. "The mayor and the others have got it all wrong. We are all very much alive."

"Is everyone here a Supernatural?" I said.

"I couldn't say," he said.

I looked Rip Van Winkle over more closely. I thought maybe he wasn't as old as I'd first thought.

"Where was I?" he asked.

"You were talking about the former librarian."

Olive brought our food out at the same time. Rip took a

big bite of his hamburger. Blood dribbled down into his beard, which made him smile.

"He had a fatal flaw," Rip Van Winkle said. "The librarian. Fatal flaw."

"What was that?"

"Bad breaker upper."

"That could be fatal," I agreed. "Sonya Wishbone mentioned the possibility."

He asked me how I'd got to Eden, and I told him about the clown. Like everyone who I told about the clown, he said that the clown was known as a bad funny man.

"He wasn't very funny," I said.

"No," he said, taking more big bites of his hamburger. "I heard he flunked out of clown college."

I asked him about the fresh graves over in the graveyard (trying to get my money's worth) and he said that those weren't people in the graves.

"What then?"

"Every once in a while, something comes down the stream from the mountain peaks and gets caught in the nets we use to catch fish. We feel the need to bury it sometimes."

"Monsters?"

He shrugged. "They live high in the mountains. Right up there on the peaks, higher than you can imagine. Don't have a name. All I can tell you is they have wings. They fall sometimes. They float down to us in the stream and we bury them."

"Angels?" I said.

"Not angels," he said. "Like I said. They don't have a name."

I asked him more about the creatures, but he couldn't tell me anything. They were always dead. He couldn't say whether they had the gift of language. Except for the wings, they looked human.

"A bad breaker upper," I said. "I can't say I'm surprised."

"I thought I might be the first to tell you."

"You could be the first to tell me he was a thief and a liar," I said.

He looked me over. "You surprise me, young fella. I can see now that I should have picked a day at least a few weeks away. My apologies."

I said I had to get back to the library.

"You watch yourself," Rip said.

"I've never understood that one," I said. "How can I watch myself? I'm going to watch others. Everyone."

"Here's a free piece of advice."

"All right." I had the feeling he didn't give much away for free.

"There's people in this town who don't want you to be the librarian. They'll be willing to get you out of town any way they have to. Buried in the cemetery or walking off into the woods. Wouldn't matter to them."

"Why?"

"You're a threat to their plans," he said, standing. "I'll walk out with you."

We walked out the front door and onto the wide sidewalk, where we walked side by side.

"What plans?"

"That's a good question. You a believer in the Christian version of things?"

"Let's say I'm not exclusive," I said.

"I'm with you there. Doesn't matter though, does it? We ended up here. Not Asgard or Elysian Fields or reincarnated as a Turkey Vulture, which wouldn't be so bad, by the way. Lots of friends. Never kill for your food. Never have to work all that hard. And they can fly."

"All true," I said. "I've thought the same thing. Also, no real predators to speak of."

"Great minds," he said. "But you and I ended up here. Cards we were dealt."

"The universe is one big poker game. That the way you see it?"

He turned down a side-street and said, "You said it, Brother. Play your cards well."

Chapter Twenty-Seven

I spent the rest of the afternoon in the library looking for evidence. I searched the computer and found the librarian had been using his personal card to check out books on black magic. I went to the second floor, and I called to the books but they didn't come to me. I looked for them on the shelves. They weren't there. In all, there were 42 books missing.

I looked for the books in the apartment and found none, and I went into the Collection of Curiosities to look for them. I tried calling for them and got no answer and then I tried looking with my third eye, but couldn't see them. So where were they?

I went back to the apartment. It took me a while, but I found the loose floorboard in the corner of the smaller bedroom and a box in a cubbyhole. I pulled the box out and at first it seemed like a solid block of wood. Then I saw the indentation for the librarian's ring. I placed it in the indentation and the box opened.

I suppose you could call it a treasure box. There was a deed to the general store and dozens of pieces of jewelry and cash. Lots of it. Thirty thousand dollars. The strangest things were receipts from hotels in Las Vegas, the most recent last month. But there were a lot of them. It appeared he visited Las Vegas about twice every month.

How?

The receipts were for hotels and restaurants. Often the receipts were for hotel room comps at casinos. Since Las Vegas casinos weren't known for random generosity, I concluded he was spending a lot gambling in those casinos. Enough that they knew him and gave him free suites.

Where had all the money come from and how had he gotten to Las Vegas to spend it twice every month? Where were the 42 books?

Chapter Twenty-Eight

That night I went to the town meeting as the mayor asked. The lights in the park at the center of the square were on. Christmas lights. There were probably fifty or sixty folding chairs up by a small stage built with large blocks of wood that had been assembled some time that day. I was told by the mayor's secretary to take a front-row seat since I'd be speaking. My palms were sweating.

By sunset, the park was filled with people. There were well over a hundred there, which was over half the town. The mayor made a speech about all the good things he was doing and all the good things he would do in the future and then he said that the church was going to be open tomorrow if anyone wanted to pray to whichever god they prayed to.

"Will there be any gods present?" someone from the audience asked.

"Not as far as I know, but as you're well aware, there are sometimes surprise guests."

Then he said that Chuck Newman was retiring as the town supply agent. He hoped some young person would take over the position. Then Chuck Newman got up on stage. He said he was only 28, which was a young age to retire, but he was lucky to be doing so. The left sleeve of his shirt was empty of the arm that should have filled it, and he wore a black patch over one eye, and one side of his face was scarred by what appeared to be burns. He limped when he walked.

"I'm sorry I can't go on," he said. "I know there are others who will want to take my position though. You do a great service for the town. Of course, most don't survive to retirement age, because as we all know, the woods are full of—"

"Thank you," the mayor said, grabbing the microphone from Chuck's hand, "for your service."

The mayor reminded the town that the supply agent only had to go to a clearing about a mile away where a helicopter would land and unload in an average of ten minutes. The pilot would have a partner who carried a shotgun.

"You won't be alone either, as Chuck has graciously agreed to go on the run with you as your shotgun support for at least one run."

Chuck pushed his way back to the microphone. He said, "At most one run."

The mayor gave him a sharp look and shoved him back. "You all know it's one of our best paying town jobs. See me afterward if you're interested."

The mayor went into a discussion about garbage pickup and the need for more townspeople to work in the garden on the north end of town during the next week. The farm, which was just south of town, also needed another worker who was familiar with farm animal care. I planned on taking a look at the farm soon. And the garden.

Lord Blackstone was the next speaker. He was holding

a Dark Arts workshop at his house this weekend. He encouraged people to come even if they didn't consider themselves evil.

"You cannot have light without the dark," he said. "We may have a surprise guest."

"Not the one-eyed witch of the woods, is it?" someone yelled.

"No inviting witches," someone else yelled.

"Not her," Lord Blackstone said. "And ten percent off for those who have never attended a Dark Arts workshop."

"You're not going to summon any demons, are you?" someone shouted.

"I won't say that we will or won't at this time. But I know a few who might be available if enough people want to hear from a demon."

After Lord Blackstone sat down, the mayor called me up and I got up on stage and introduced myself as the new librarian. I'd barely said ten words before stars fell from the sky. Or pieces of stars anyway.

At first I thought that someone was setting off fireworks, but then I saw that the explosions of light were actually falling from the sky.

"Take cover," the mayor yelled from the stage.

People did not need to be told twice. They ran for it. Some of these bits of whatever caught trees on fire. I could see some landing on homes, but the fire didn't catch. Pails of water were being passed to put out the places where fire had caught. I could see that there was a team responsible for this. I imagined them working on drills to become efficient at fire management. They worked well together.

Olive came up beside me. She took my arm.

"Come on," she said.

But before we could move, the fire stopped falling from the sky and an old man with a long beard appeared.

"I do love a good entrance," he said.

Everyone stopped moving.

"Down on your knees, humans," he said. "I am god."

"Well, maybe, a god," someone shouted.

Some got down on their knees, but most didn't. Neither Olive nor I went to our knees. The whole worshiping god thing just seemed so last century to me. It wasn't that I didn't believe in the universe and in some kind of order beyond my comprehension; I just found old bearded gods hard to worship.

"It's this way everywhere now," the god said. "Even when I put on a good show. That's fire falling from the sky, people. What more do you want? But does everyone go down on their knees and start wailing like they did in the old days? No."

He looked ready to set us all on fire.

"We don't doubt your power," I said. "You could probably wipe us out with a sweep of your arm."

"I could," he said.

"But that wouldn't make you a god."

"What more do you want?" he said.

"Nothing, Great One," someone shouted, someone on their knees.

"Nothing," he said, disgusted. He looked around. More than half were not on their knees. "Tell me the truth, librarian."

"We need more from a god. We aren't primitives anymore. We need more sophisticated gods now."

"How about I show you sophisticated and turn the sky to fire and burn you and everyone in this little Podunk town to ashes."

"Again," I said, "impressive. You certainly are impressive. But we need someone all-knowing. Someone who can give us a good afterlife story. Someone who created us. Someone who can show us the mysteries of the universe. All those things and more."

"I really should just light you all on fire," he said.

He stroked his beard. He did look like a god. You had to give him that.

"You want too much," he said. "I won't be back."

Then he disappeared. And so, another god fell by the roadside of human evolution.

The mayor decided that the meeting was over and told everyone to go home. People argued about whether they had just seen a god or demon or powerful wizard or itinerant magician. There were a lot of different possibilities put forward.

The townspeople wandered off toward home. Some seemed shaken, but others seemed defiant. A fight broke out between two men. The constable called for help to break it up from some of the younger men in town. They helped him, but bloodied up some townspeople in the process.

"Let's go over to the bar," Olive said.

As we walked over, she said, "Your first god?"

"He was."

"What did you think?"

"Seemed a little testy."

"More and more of them are that way now. Hard to find worshipers. I think they feel they've lost their purpose."

I thought about telling her about Karl. I could use her perspective. But I felt it might ruin things.

We walked into the bar.

Ryan and Camila were already there, and we sat with them.

"Some fire rain, wasn't it?" Ryan said.

"That's not what it was," Camila said.

"Celestial rain," I said.

"What?" Olive said.

"Like rain from heaven?" Ryan said.

"He was just a small god throwing his weight around," Camila said. "It was a meteor shower was all it was."

The fire team had put out the many little fires around town. I wouldn't mind joining the fire team if I ended up staying for a while.

"How did you two get here?" I asked. "I mean to Eden."

"We were hiking," Ryan said.

"And someone got us lost," Camila said.

"Which was lucky because some weird shit was happening," Ryan said.

"Luck had nothing to do with it," Camila said. "It was your map reading skills that got us lost in the first place."

"What kind of weird shit?" I asked.

"We were walking along and parts of us would disappear. Like a hand. A leg. They'd just become invisible. And then I saw a fog moving in and I knew when it came over us we'd disappear entirely."

"You didn't know anything," Camila said. "It was a prediction based on a pretty weak assumption."

"Parts of us were disappearing," he said.

"That's true, but you're always jumping to conclusions."

I wished I hadn't got them talking about it.

"We'd better get going," Camila said. "We've got school tomorrow."

"School?"

"Walter likes to teach us science three mornings a week. Gives us homework. Tomorrow it's The History of Science. Other days it's work in the lab. Chemistry. Robotics."

The Librarian of The Haunted Library

"He is brilliant," Camila said. "Before he came here, he was teaching at MIT and then started his own company with a group of scientists."

"Doing shady things for the government," Ryan said.

"You don't know that," she said.

They were still arguing as they left. I watched them go out the door.

Olive said, "They're an opposites attract couple."

We talked about them. She said they argued just about every time she saw them. Sometimes it got uncomfortable.

"Want to walk me home," she said, "to the haunted house?"

"Is it really haunted?"

"Yes and no," she said.

"So, it's haunted."

"A dead person lives there, but he's not haunting it."

I said I wanted to walk her home. I asked the waiter if I could run a tab and he said I could because I was the librarian, and he sincerely hoped I would continue to be the librarian for the next six days.

Another pool contestant.

He gave me the check, and I added a tip and signed it.

We walked outside. There was the smell of burnt wood and flora in the air. We walked down Main Street toward the corner where Olive lived.

"I think it's best I'm upfront with you," Olive said. "I don't want to be one of those couples like Ryan and Camila who seem to get off on conflict."

"Are we a couple?" I said, amused and flattered, so two good feelings.

"We will be," she said. "I mean, it looks that way."

"You can see that it looks that way?"

"I get feelings."

"And you feel us being a couple?"

"But not like them."

"Okay."

"It's not that I mind a good argument. I just like to save them for special occasions. I don't enjoy going around looking for them every moment."

"Did you know we were going to be a couple when you told me I should leave town?" I said.

"Potentially," she said. "I still thought you should leave. Being a librarian is dangerous."

"Now you think we'll be a couple?"

"We're in the awkward phase. We're almost a couple."

"But," I said, "you know I'm leaving. I need to be honest, too. I will move on. Maybe as soon as I find out who killed the librarian. Even if I stay, it won't be for long. You understand that, right?"

"I understand. Do you?"

"Only about half the time," I admitted and thought maybe I was exaggerating.

We came to her house on the corner. Massive and dark.

"It's my father," she said.

"What?"

"The dead person. Sort of. He died, but he woke up before I could bury him."

"Lucky for him."

"He was always a lucky man. Is. Anyway, he's living in the house with me."

"So, when you said you lived with your father—"

"I do live with him. He's just not alive. It doesn't stop us from getting along."

"But when it comes to changing a light bulb—"

"Not a chance," she said. "The dead and electricity do not go together."

"Still, it's probably nice to have him around," I said.

"I think it might cause problems, him being dead, at some point. He thinks maybe it was some kind of clerical error."

"Stranger things have happened," I said from experience.

"Every day," she said.

"If we're going to be a couple," I said. "I should be able to kiss you good night."

"You should, eventually," she said and walked away.

After about a dozen steps, she stopped and asked me if I wanted to come over for dinner tomorrow night.

"Sure," I said.

We said good night again, and I started walking to the library

I heard a sound of footsteps. It seemed like they were trying to sneak up on me. I swung around. Nothing was there, but I still felt a presence.

Silence.

And then whatever it was — and given this town, it could have been many things — disappeared.

Chapter Twenty-Nine

"Whooooooooooooooooooo," I heard as I came into the library and locked the door behind me.

"Cut it out," I said.

The ghost appeared.

"Do you really have to do that?" I said.

"The library likes it. Makes it feel protected."

That seemed suspect to me. The library didn't really like or dislike things. It wasn't alive. Unless it was.

He said, "You're a fast worker. You already have a girlfriend."

"How do you even know about that?"

"You were thinking about it when you walked in."

"You can read my mind?" I said.

"No," he said.

I tried to block him from reading my mind. I thought of a wall around my thoughts. A high stone wall like around a castle.

"Can't read you at all now," he said. "Good to have someone to weep at your funeral, though."

The Librarian of The Haunted Library

"You see me dying?"

"You don't think you're going to die?" he said.

"I mean soon? You see my funeral soon?"

"I haven't seen it," he said.

"Most of the townspeople seem to think I won't last long."

He shrugged. "I haven't looked so I haven't seen. You could die in the next minute. It wouldn't surprise me. Of course, few things do after all I've seen."

I walked away. He followed me. His feet did not have to touch the ground. I would like that. I wondered if someday I would be a ghost.

I walked down the stairs toward my apartment. The ghost followed.

"Have you heard of Cousin Deadeye?" I asked.

"Yes," he said. "A duke of hell if I'm not mistaken."

"He's here in the woods. He took the teenagers. Now he's made some deal with them, I think."

"Bad news for the teenagers and the town."

"You can say that again."

"Bad news for the teenagers and the town."

"Did you know the librarian was stealing books?"

"No," he said.

"And taking trips to Las Vegas."

"I suspected that he was up to something, but he and I were unable to converse. I found him difficult to watch, so I didn't."

He stopped in front of my apartment.

"Why did you find him difficult to watch?"

"Let's just say the man was a buffoon. He never should have been a librarian."

"I'd invite you in," I said, "but the place is a mess."

"Don't trust me?" he said.

"Nothing personal," I said.

"I understand."

"The librarian wasn't killed by the teenagers," I said. "I've decided they're innocent."

"That's four people in town it wasn't then," the ghost said.

"He was a bad man," I said. "The librarian. He was a terrible man. Maybe I should just let it go."

"You won't," he said.

Chapter Thirty

The next morning, I woke up, and it was close to nine o'clock. Not enough time to go to the café for breakfast. I made some coffee and opened the library. I read a novel for a while. It seemed like a long time since I'd been in a story. Normally I read a novel or two a week.

The mayor came into the library while the book club was in a fierce argument because some thought that 42 as the meaning of life, the universe, and everything was ridiculous and others thought it was just as likely as anything else.

"Spirited group, aren't they?" the mayor said.

At that moment, two gray-haired ladies in dresses and pumps and pearl necklaces circled each other like they were about to go into MMA grappling. One of them tried and failed to get a takedown.

"They're passionate about books," I said.

The other one shoved her back, and they circled each other again.

"You take down like a grandma," one said.

"I am a grandma," her opponent said. "And so are you."

They stopped circling. They both looked stricken.

"Sorry, dear, I get reckless with my trash talk."

"I like being a grandma," the first one said, nearly in tears.

"Me too."

"I miss my grandchildren."

They were both near tears and then they apologized and hugged each other and went back to their chairs.

"Are you settling into the job?" the mayor asked.

"I think I might be," I said. I surprised myself. I didn't really settle. I was pathologically unsettled. I kept my bags packed. Of course, this time I didn't have any bags, so it would have to be more of a metaphor than physical reality, anyway.

"That's good."

"But I haven't changed my mind about staying. I'll still be moving on as soon as I've done what I need to do."

"You're a traveling man."

"That's right."

"What is it you need to do?" he asked. "From your perspective? Besides, find the librarian's murderer."

"I don't know. I'll know when I've done it."

"So it's more of a feeling you get?"

"Right."

"Fine," he said. "Good to know. Just give me some warning when you get the feeling, please."

"Sure."

"I'm afraid I have some bad news. Mrs. Wishbone is dead. You visited her yesterday and today she's dead. If I didn't know better, I'd think you were bad luck. Wait, I don't know better. Are you bad luck?"

"I don't think so," I said.

"Doc thinks she died of old age. It happens to the elderly, apparently."

"But he's not sure?" I said.

"Not yet."

"Is he checking for poison?"

"Of course," he said. "The Doc always checks for poison."

"I bet it beats out cancer and heart attacks here in Eden," I said.

"I'd better get to work," he said. "It's the busy time of year."

"It is?"

"It's always the busy time of year," he said.

I thought that kind of defeated the use of the word busy, but I didn't say anything.

The book club calmed down and settled into a discussion about what their next selection should be. It was between a Terry Pratchett novel and *The Stand*. Couldn't go wrong with either, in my opinion.

At eleven, I had to ask them to leave. They decided to continue the discussion at the café over an early lunch. I checked out two copies of *The Stand* to two of the book club members, so I saw the way the debate was leaning.

I closed the library and went to talk to Doc. By the time I got to his office, he'd changed into his undertaker clothes and was working on the body in the basement where he had his undertaker tools.

"She didn't die of old age, did she?" I said.

"Another poisoning. Seems we're having an outbreak."

"Same poison?"

"Yes."

"Same poisoner or someone who wants us to think it's the same poisoner."

"Your area of expertise," he said. "I just save them and then, in my other position, bury them."

A bit of an exaggeration all around, I thought. I sniffed her face.

"In her tea, wasn't it?" I said.

"Seems so," he said.

"Cherry. Someone who came after I was at her house last night. Someone she knew."

"It's a small town."

"I mean really knew; not just small town knew. Trusted. Someone who made tea for her."

"A woman," the Doc said.

"Poison is usually a woman's method of murder," I said.

"Not in this town," Doc said. "Everyone seems fond of it. I mean, everyone who murders someone."

I thanked Doc and left.

Chapter Thirty-One

I decided to go to the town cemetery to think. Cemeteries had always been good places for me. They were quiet. I thought that the person who'd murdered Mrs. Wishbone had wasted a murder. They thought she was going to tell me something. She hadn't, and I doubted she would.

I noticed a few of the graves had been dug up. My first thought was grave robbers. Which seemed unlikely since the profession had gone out with the Victorian age.

Three graves had been dug up.

I leaned over and looked into one of the graves. The coffin was open. No one home. The other two were the same. It was troubling.

"Looks like we've got some corpses out for a walk about," Lord Blackstone said. He was leaning against a large pine tree. He looked relaxed.

"Or someone dug them up," I said. "Woke them."

"Who would do that?" he said.

I knelt down and picked up a handful of grave dirt. I

put it in my pocket. You never knew when grave dirt might come in handy.

"Someone who can wake the dead. A necromancer maybe. Know any?"

"It's a messy business waking the dead," he said, ignoring my question.

I stood up. Lord Blackstone's eyes were very attentive. He was not one to look away. I wish he had been.

"I met a necromancer once," I said. "Down along the border near El Paso."

"Is that right?" he said.

"His name was Alberto."

"Mexican?" he said.

"A coyote. He'd kill the Mexicans before he sneaked them across the Rio Grande and then wake them on the other side. Then he would claim they'd been born in the United States."

"Who would believe that?"

"International Supernatural Law states that someone who is raised by a necromancer in a country other than that of their origin is considered to be born again in said country he or she is raised in. So, the ISL agents would get him the papers. It's a loophole."

"Outrageous. This is what's destroying this country. Immigrants who are so desperate they're willing to be killed and raised from the dead just to get into America ought to be sent back to Mexico."

"Alberto said he could charge more because of the papers. When he woke them, they owed him their lives. He'd put a little makeup on them and no one would notice. You know how people are. They don't really look closely at strangers."

"Charming story."

"One thing about Alberto. He was very neat. He said most necromancers were. Had to be detail oriented to wake someone from the dead properly."

"You're saying this was an amateur here?"

"Looks that way to me. I'd say this is more likely the work of a spell witch."

He shrugged. "I'm sure they'll turn up somewhere."

"You know who was buried here?"

"Someone of no consequence from the looks of things."

"Right."

"It's a little town. People get bored."

"And dig up graves?"

"Tell me you didn't dig up a grave or two when you were a teenager."

"I didn't dig up a grave or two when I was a teenager."

He shook his head. "You're like that boy with his finger in the dam. Sooner or later, it will break open and you will be washed away by what is on the other side."

I'd heard this before. It must be taught at Dark Arts School.

"What is on the other side?"

"The Dark." he said, pushing off the pine tree to stand up straight.

We stared at each other. I was taking his measure. I'd say 40 long. I'd worked in a Men's clothing store for two weeks once.

"I can find out from the mayor who was buried in the grave," I said. "You might as well tell me."

He sighed. "My wife's poor relations. Cousins."

I looked back at the town. It was like many towns in some ways. It had secrets. Of course, it was unlike many towns in other ways. People generally didn't go around digging up graves and raising the dead. I would have noticed.

"Your daughter seems troubled," I said.

He shrugged. "She's a teenager."

But there was a lot in that shrug if you knew how to read shrugs. Unfortunately, I didn't.

"You ended up here when you were running away from the law," I said. "What were they after you for?"

"How do you know that?"

I almost said "I'm the librarian" just to mess with him, but I didn't. I had looked him up. There was a database of people who lived in Eden and a brief bio of each. I thought the former librarian had put it together or at least added to it, but there was an entry for me. Who did that? As far as I could remember, not me.

"Murder?" I said.

"That's not your concern."

"The Supernatural Spooks were after you, right?" I said.

That's what the entry had said. I'd never heard of the Supernatural Spooks, but apparently there was a sort of police force that took care of certain crimes done by Supernaturals. I'd need to find out more about that.

"It's been taken care of."

"Sure," I said. "The way rich people in all the worlds take care of things, right? Bought your way out."

"It wasn't murder," he said. "Just a little misunderstanding between an Earl and myself. All settled. If you think you can use that, you're mistaken. We in the party of the Dark Arts are united against forces trying to work against us."

"You heard Mrs. Wishbone was murdered?" I said.

I could tell he had by the lack of surprise in his face.

"News travels fast in a one-horse town," he said.

Technically, it didn't even have one horse. Which did bother me. Why no horses or dogs? I'd never been able to have a dog, but I'd always wanted one.

"I want to go to your tower," I said.

"Why?"

"I think there's something there for me."

"I can't imagine what."

"Fed-Ex package?"

"Doubtful," he said.

I didn't know what was there, but I felt something was. Sometimes there was a reason for such a feeling. Once I had been in Iowa on a farm and I went to a barn to search for a murder weapon. It was what cops called a hunch. Only later I realized that I'd noticed a single piece of straw on the murderer's shirt. Turned out, the murder weapon was in the barn; he'd killed his wife with a pitchfork. There was a case of instinct being strongly enhanced by an observation. Sometimes, though, it was just as random as a tornado landing or the fact that avocados are not considered a vegetable but a berry fruit.

"Will you take me?" I said.

"When?"

"Now."

"All right," he said.

"I do have to be back by tonight," I said. "I'm having dinner at Olive's."

"No promises," he said.

Words with a definite ominous echo given the source and circumstance.

Chapter Thirty-Two

We walked out of town and down the path into the woods. He led the way. The monkeys were at it again in the trees. They sounded like they were fans of opposing football teams, cheering and jeering and tossing off the occasional insult to the other side.

"Are those your monkeys?" I shouted.

"They're their own monkeys. We call them whisper monkeys."

"Misnomer, if I ever heard one," I said.

We came to a split in the path. We went right. I couldn't see the tower. We were in tall leafy trees.

"Many of the old fairytales have them," he said.

The monkeys became silent all of a sudden. I looked up, and they were gone.

"Perhaps we should increase our speed," Lord Blackstone said.

"Why?" I said.

"Never good when the monkeys disappear. It means something is coming, usually something large and dangerous."

A lion came wandering down the trail toward us. A large lion. My finely honed instinct said dangerous.

"That isn't supposed to be here," I said, but then I remembered I didn't know where here was.

"An African lion," Lord Blackstone said. "He is magnificent, isn't he?"

"How did an African lion get here?" I asked Lord Blackstone.

He gave me a look like that was a stupid question, so I answered it myself.

"He walked."

"That is a creature of substance," he said, pulling out a wand.

He was a wand magician. That was good to know.

The lion roared.

I didn't have my sword. That seemed like a major oversight.

"I suppose you can turn him into a mouse?" I said hopefully.

He shook his head. "That's a myth. It's extremely hard to turn anything into anything else, but a lion is royalty. Nearly impossible."

The lion was looking at us in a way that made me very uncomfortable. Sort of like Rip Van Winkle had looked at his hamburger in Lucy's before he took his first bite.

"You're going to try to kill it, anyway, right?" I said.

"It's bad luck to kill a king."

There was no good place to have bad luck, but a haunted forest seemed particularly bad.

"Are you familiar with the story of two monks coming down a mountain?" I said.

He shrugged. It was like someone speaking a foreign

language to me. I would know if he had or hadn't if I could read shrugs, but I couldn't.

"Two monks are coming down a mountain. They come around a corner and they see a tiger. The tiger is ten feet away from them. One monk says to the other, 'Brother, we must face our death with good grace. We cannot outrun a tiger.' The other monk looks at him and says, '"Brother, I do not have to outrun a tiger. I just have to outrun you."'

The lion roared and crouched as if it was about to leap.

"Shake the monkey tree," I said to Lord Blackstone.

He raised his wand and whispered a spell, and the tree shook. Two whisper monkeys landed right in front of the lion. They ran. One was faster than the other. He got away. The other was dinner.

Lord Blackstone and I rested for a moment to catch our breaths. Then we went on. About twenty minutes later, we were climbing the stairs of his tower.

"Why are we here, librarian?" he asked.

"The view," I said.

We had gone up a few hundred steps, and I could see we had hundreds more to go up.

"You won't be able to see anything off my tower unless you have darkness in you"

"I'll be able to see," I said.

He looked me over. "Perhaps I've misjudged you."

"You didn't kill the librarian, did you?" I said.

"We were in business together. Why would I kill him?"

"He probably slept with your wife at one time or another."

"If I killed everyone in town who slept with my wife, there would hardly be anyone left."

"Would you tell me if you had killed him?"

"Of course not," he said.

He was honest about being dishonest.

"What business were you in?" I asked.

"Our business."

"Make a lot of money?"

"Some here, some there."

"You can still return those late books," I said. "Save you some fines."

"I don't have any books," he said.

We reached the next landing. A woman wearing funeral weeds met us. Somehow, the tower swelled out and there were several rooms. It was like the library. A kind of magic I couldn't identify.

"My mother," Lord Blackstone said. "Lady Blackstone."

"A pleasure to meet you," I said.

"My son keeps me here. That's how evil he is. Locks his own mother up in a tower. I'm so proud."

She laughed. It was an evil laugh. We said our goodbyes and kept going up the stairs.

After a few more floors, I asked, "Does she know?"

"That she's dead? No. I see no reason to tell her."

I knew he was planning on pushing me off the roof when we got to the top. I'd have to convince him not to before we got there. It was a very long way down.

Chapter Thirty-Three

As we walked up the stairs, I told him about meeting Cousin Deadeye in a town in Vermont where he was calling himself Darkheart.

"Seemed a little on the nose to me," I said.

"They say he's a master at converting humans to our side. He has more converts than any other demon. Has won salesman of the year for the last hundred running."

"I got in his way," I said.

"I don't believe you. If you had, you'd be dead."

"Karl wouldn't allow it."

"Really? Why is that?"

"He thinks I'm his son."

Lord Blackstone frowned. "Why would he think that?"

"Because I'm his son."

"That's preposterous."

"I'm the white sheep of the family. I only found out recently myself. Believe me, it was a shock."

He watched me closely. I whispered to him. "I'm telling you the truth."

We got to the top.

"How do I know you're telling the truth?"

"You know," I said.

I realized he did the way I realized some things. Intuition or its big brother letting me know something I couldn't really know. He must have once heard a rumor, about me. He'd discounted it. Now he had to reconsider.

"I could still throw you off the roof. Karl might not know who was responsible."

"It's a haunted wood. Someone or some thing would tell him sooner or later. Could be a career ender, even a life ender, for you."

"You are beginning to annoy me," he said.

I looked around. "Nice view."

He shrugged. "For someone who knows how to look. You don't."

I tried to see with my third eye and I did see. "It's the whole world down there, isn't it?"

"Bits of it," he said in a pouty voice.

Then I saw the telescope. It was over in the corner. The light had to hit it a certain way, or it was hidden.

"I'd like to look through the telescope," I said.

He seemed disappointed that I'd been able to see it.

"You belong in the Dark Arts Society," he said. "You can't see the telescope without darkness. And if Karl is your father, you are—you have to be one of us."

"Maybe I'll join," I said. "But for now, I want to look through the telescope."

I went over to it and leaned down and looked through the eyepiece. I couldn't see anything but darkness.

Lord Blackstone coughed. He nodded toward the silver slot under the viewer. It had a sign next to it, 25 cents. I felt in my pocket.

"Do you have a quarter you could lend me?" I asked Lord Blackstone.

He sighed. He pulled a quarter out and handed it to me. "Thank you."

I put the quarter in the slot and looked through the telescope.

I passed over a flood of images. It was too much to see. The whole world. I tried using my third eye. I saw a woman giving birth in a small, dirty hotel room.

"Why am I seeing a woman giving birth?" I asked.

"It zooms in where it thinks you want it to zoom."

My third eye had chosen her for a reason.

The image disappeared after five seconds, but I knew whose birth I was seeing. The woman's face was hidden by long black hair and the obvious extreme pain of childbirth, but it was her. I felt a tightness in my chest.

I was right. I would know it was her if I saw her.

"Not much help," I lied.

"Maybe you don't have enough darkness," he said, hopefully.

"Maybe not," I said.

"Can you see all the way back to the beginning with your telescope?" I asked him.

"No one can see all the way back. Not even the gods. Not even Karl."

"Do you have another quarter?" I said. I wanted to focus the telescope on the town of Eden.

"Sorry," he said.

"Really?"

"I'm out of quarters."

We went down the stairs. It was faster and easier than going up.

The Librarian of The Haunted Library

"Do you know why Cousin Deadeye took your daughter?" I asked.

"He had his reasons."

"You'd better be careful," I said. "He's the worst of the worst."

"That's high praise."

"Sorry you didn't get to kill me on your tower," I said.

"No need to apologize. I'll have another chance."

We passed by the apartment with his mother in it. She was watching TV. She didn't even acknowledge us.

We walked down the stairs and back through the woods.

"What were you and the former librarian really arguing about?" I asked as we neared Eden.

"Women," he said.

I thought I might be just about ready to have an argument about women. But I wasn't going to have this argument with another man. I was going to have it with a woman. Much more dangerous.

Chapter Thirty-Four

That night I went to Olive's at the appointed time, which was seven. I was nervous for more than one reason. I walked up the sidewalk to the red brick house. What was on my mind was a question. But it was a dangerous question and the answer might be more dangerous still.

There was a nice front porch with chairs and a porch swing. It faced east. I thought it would be a good place to have a cup of coffee in the morning. Of course, there would be a dead father walking around, so that might put a bit of a damper on sunrise. I didn't know exactly what kind of dead he'd be, having never met anyone who came back from death who wasn't a ghost. And, really, they hadn't come back, at least not all the way. If he was a zombie, then most likely Olive was his caregiver as much as a daughter.

Olive answered the door. We hugged.

"I'm glad you came," she said.

The hug surprised me in a good way.

"Me too," I said.

"I need to talk to you after dinner. Something I should have told you before now."

I liked and dreaded the sound of that.

We went down a hallway, holding hands, passing a large study and a smaller sitting room. The house was both elegant and comfortable. I'd been in only one other like this, a professor who taught at Harvard. He'd given me a ride from St. Louis to Boston and ended up offering me a place to stay for a few days. He thought I was wasting my abilities and wanted to help me get a college degree.

I left after a day. No word to him. The best I could do was write a note that I was sorry. He was looking for someone to fall in love with, and I wasn't that person. I was probably looking for a father figure, so whatever relationship we ended up having wouldn't satisfy either of us.

The dining room table was a nice one with a tablecloth and silver eating utensils.

"This is my father, Doctor Hanover," Olive said.

He looked pale and ashen. Death would do that to skin. He wore gloves. He apologized for wearing them.

"Bit of flesh falling off in places," he said. "Curse of being dead."

I shook hands with him and said I was pleased to meet him.

It turned out he wasn't a medical doctor, but a PhD. Like the Harvard professor, he taught history. American history, in his case, the Revolutionary War. A woman came in carrying a silver tray with drinks.

"Hope you don't mind," Olive said. "I know you like gin and tonics, so I had Elaine make you one. This is Elaine, by the way. She's my father's housekeeper."

"Slave," she said, and set drinks in front of each of us. The word made me immediately uncomfortable. She didn't say it with venom or even anger, just stated it like it was a fact.

"Please, Elaine," Doctor Hanover said.

"Yes, Master," she said.

I looked at Olive, who shrugged.

"Elaine saw a hypnotist at last year's fair and he put her under," Professor Hanover said. "She's very susceptible."

"First she quacked like a duck," Olive said.

"I did no such thing," Elaine said.

"He convinced her that I am a former Egyptian King; furthermore, she was one of my slaves. She has decided that she is still my slave. I'd fire her; however, given my condition, it's difficult to find help."

"You can't fire a slave," she said. "There's not much good about being a slave, but that's one thing. Anyway, you're right. No one wants to work for a dead man."

"Prejudice is a difficult thing to get past," he said.

"Tell me about it," Elaine said.

Over the course of the meal, which was very good, I learned that the professor retired from teaching at 62 to travel around the world. He met a woman thirty years his junior, and they travelled together for a while and became friends and then lovers. Her name was Constance. They married and continued on with their travels.

"We were very close to completing our circumnavigation of the globe. We were in the rainforest in Maui. We'd lived in many places by then, spent the better part of a decade on our travels. Then we got lost on a simple trip through the forest and ended up in the haunted woods. We were separated in some caves and my daughter and I never saw my wife again."

"These haunted woods sure do get around," I said.

"I have a theory that there are doors, or perhaps more

like halls, that are all over the world. Who put them there and the reason they exist at all is unclear. However, people stumble into them. Most of them never get out of the haunted forest. Only a few make it to Eden."

"I'm sorry," I said.

"We looked for my wife. The librarian and I went out into the woods a day after we arrived, but on our third trip out we nearly didn't make it back. He refused to go out again."

"Headhunters," I said. "Olive told me."

"These are not your ancestors' haunted woods. There are many more dangers than witches with gingerbread houses and preheated stoves."

"I'm sorry," I said again.

We were finished eating and went into the living room. He called it the parlor. He lit up a small cigar.

"Daddy," Olive said.

"What's it going to do, kill me?" he said, chuckling. Professors, in my experience, tended to chuckle.

The doctor looked at me and offered me what he called a cigarillo and I would have liked to take it, but I could tell from Olive's look that it would be a foolish move.

"No thanks," I said.

He asked me if it was true I'd met the one-eyed witch of the woods and I said I had. He wanted to know how I survived her.

"Most don't," he said.

"She was afraid of the town."

"No, that's not it," he said.

"And I had the sword from the collection of curiosities. But mainly I think she wanted me to take the teens home. Maybe afraid she'd give into temptation and kill them and the town would come after her."

"It was the sword," he said.

We talked about other things.

"You've travelled," my daughter tells me.

"All over the country many times," I said

"Why?"

"I'm not sure."

"You have a purpose," he said. "It's not just random."

I told him about the mission messages that came to me from dreams, strangers, even animals, and then I told him I felt the road was the first home I'd ever had.

"How about now?" Olive said. "Are you supposed to be here?"

"I guess," I said. "It started with being told about the clown. I guess that led me here."

"I'll go get us coffee," she said.

"Most of the Librarians have been magicians," Doctor Hanover said. He told me about a few of them.

"I'm not," I said.

"I can see that; however, you are something, aren't you? What?"

"Enough interrogation," Olive said, coming in with the coffee.

"Sorry," he said. "I'm very sorry. It's an old habit. Trying to dig the truth out from hidden places. Historians need that skill."

He stood and said it was a pleasure to meet me. It was time for him to retire to his library and work on his book.

"What's it called?"

"The book of Death," he said. "I want to write about what it's like to die and the memories I have of life. Unfortunately, I can't write about what everyone wants to know the most. Where do we go, if anywhere, after we die? In my case, I went back to life before I had any of those answers. I'm like everyone else, still left to wonder."

"Writing that book is going to be the death of you," Olive said, smiling at him.

He smiled back.

"Excuse us," he said. "We have a lot of low death humor in this house. I suppose it's unavoidable. I believe someday soon I will be taken. Some bureaucrat will get in touch with Death and point out the obvious fact. They missed someone. And he'll come for me."

"I hope it's a long time in the future," I said.

"Not I," he said.

"Father," Olive said.

He shrugged. "Was that inappropriate? Sorry. I can't tell sometimes. One effect of my condition. But the truth is, I'm ready to die properly. I'd just like to get my Olive settled first. Good night."

He left. Olive handed me the cup of coffee. Here was the moment of truth. Was it poisoned? I sniffed it.

"He sometimes might seem a bit disconnected from life because he is, well, disconnected."

She asked if I wanted to sit outside. I said I did. We went out onto the front porch and sat in deck chairs. The night smelled sweet. So did the coffee. Before I took a sip, I said, "I need to ask you something. Why did you lie to me about the librarian? I know you had an affair with him."

"I didn't lie to you. I didn't really know the man. I didn't have an affair with him. I slept with him once and that was that."

"You were angry after it ended?"

"Not me."

"Angry enough to poison him? You gave him tea. I saw you serve it to him."

I hadn't meant for it all to come out all at once like that. I felt like I'd vomited on my lap. I was embarrassed.

She looked at the coffee in my hand.

"Don't let your coffee get cold," she said.

"Seems like most of the women in town fell for him."

"Do you trust me?"

"Of course, I do," I said. "I just need you to tell me the truth."

"Take a sip of your coffee."

"I've heard he was a bad breaker upper."

"Can't start a relationship without trust," she said. "It's not possible. One sip."

I put the cup to my lips, but I couldn't do it. I couldn't be sure. She stared at me. Her eyes were so sad.

"I'd like you to leave now," she said.

"Olive—"

"Please," she said.

I got up and walked out of the house. The relationship hadn't even got going. If it was a car, it was still parked in the garage. Was the garage door even open? Was I really comparing a relationship to a car in a garage?

We hadn't even kissed. It was hardly even a relationship. I hadn't messed up a love affair because it wasn't even an affair yet.

Why then did it feel like I'd lost something important, something I already cared about? I tried to reason with myself, but I was having none of me. Sometimes it just has to hurt.

Chapter Thirty-Five

When I got back to the library, I went upstairs into the back room where the books on psychology and magic were. I tried to clear my mind and when I was focused, I called for the Ghoul. I figured since I could call for books in the library, I might be able to call for ghosts and ghouls. She appeared as Mrs. Johnson. She didn't look surprised I was calling her.

"I knew you weren't gone," I said.

"You're just saying that."

"No, I knew. I read up on you."

"I could have killed you."

"You wanted to be sure."

"Very good," she said, and she took her true form.

One cyclops eye, pointy ears, smooth, hairless gray skin, head touching the ten-foot ceiling, wide as a Mini, both male and female genitals. Pretty clearly a monster by human standards, but he/she did have a winning smile.

"Are you sure?" I said.

"I'm much older than the Christians, but I do know Karl and the fallen angels, and I don't want to get involved in that mythology. I have enough to worry about with my own. If there's to be a war between the kingdoms of Heaven and Hell, I'd prefer not to be involved. If you're the one who is prophesied to begin the battle, I will not kill you."

"Let Olive do your work?"

"Who?"

"You hoped someone else would poison me."

"I'd prefer to get my fee. But not if it drags me into something. Karl is a formidable angel, fallen or not."

"Who hired you?"

"I don't kill and tell," she said. "Even if I don't kill."

"It wasn't an angel who sent you," I said.

"Goodbye librarian," she said. "Perhaps we will meet again."

She/he/them disappeared.

I went to bed. I slept soundly. Mostly.

Chapter Thirty-Six

The next morning, before the library opened, I went to talk to Angela Morgan. I rang her doorbell. She opened the door and told me to come in. I followed her into the kitchen. She looked very pale.

"Bit under the weather," she said.

"Sorry," I said.

"It will pass."

She sat at the little table and motioned for me to sit across from her.

"Upset about the death of the librarian, no doubt," I said.

"What gives you that idea?"

"Old Mrs. Wishbone told me you were in love."

"Love?" she said bitterly. "I was in love with him, but he was never in love with me."

"All the fuss you and he made to hide your affair. Why bother?"

"His idea to keep up our little performance. He loved to perform and trick people. But what I didn't know at the time was he was tricking me. He was seeing two other women and getting money from Sonya and Olive."

"And now she's been poisoned," I said.

"What?" She wasn't faking it. She was honestly surprised and upset by the news.

"Murdered."

"But that's not possible. Sonya—who would—why?"

"I think because I went and talked to her," I said. "Someone was afraid she told me something."

She hesitated.

"Sonya was broke," she said. "Barry got everything."

"How?"

"She gave it to him. He charmed us all."

"So she was desperate," I said.

"She was desperate," she said. "She was a foolish old woman."

"Who tried to blackmail the wrong person," I said.

She stood up and escorted me out without saying another word.

She didn't need to.

Chapter Thirty-Seven

I went downstairs into the library's curious things collection and got the librarian's sword, which I wore over my shoulder like before. Then I walked over to the mayor's and told him what I was planning to do. I hoped he'd try to talk me out of it, but he didn't. He told me to be careful, which he knew was impossible because being careful would mean staying in town, and I'd just told him I was going to leave.

It was time to open the library, but I wasn't going to open it. Strike one, I guess. I went over to Olive's house even though I knew she wouldn't be there. I knocked on the door and Elaine answered, and I asked her if I could talk to the professor.

"He ain't here," she said.

"Do you know where he is?"

"Yes I do," she said.

I waited. She stared at me and I stared at her.

"Can you tell me?"

"I'm not supposed to. But the truth is I have some laundry to do. So, if you were to step into the hall closet and find the secret door, which isn't very secret, and go down the stairs to the secret cellar, which isn't very secret, and find the professor if he happened to be down there, I wouldn't know."

"Thank you."

"Don't thank me," she said.

I waited until she had walked down the hall.

I went to the closet and opened the door, and went inside. The door was easy to find. I just had to slide coats to the wall. I went down the steep, narrow stairs.

The cellar was dark. A man-cave and the man in the cave was sitting at a dining table eating. I thought this was strange, but I had noticed he didn't eat anything at dinner. I just thought it was because he was dead and it was actually because he was dead, just not the way I thought. Not because dead people don't eat, but because dead people who were zombies didn't eat cooked food.

He was munching on someone's arm.

"Hello librarian," he said, speaking with his mouth full.

"Sir," I said.

He had blood stains around his lips. He was chewing.

"Nice man cave," I said.

"Elaine won't allow me to eat upstairs anymore. It grosses her out. I do use a napkin."

I saw that he had a cloth napkin tucked into the top of his button shirt.

"Whose arm?" I asked.

"It's the former librarian's. He won't be needing it anymore. I have to be honest; it gives me some pleasure to eat him. He was a terrible man. I froze the rest of him."

"He was blackmailing Olive. I came to ask you why but I think I've got my answer."

The Librarian of The Haunted Library

He nodded. "I've been a burden to my daughter. That is unforgivable."

"How, if you don't mind my asking, did this happen?"

"We had a voodoo priestess in town for a few months, about two years ago. She planned on raising an army and taking control of the town, but the librarian at the time managed to slay her before she really got going. I'm the last of her zombies."

"Barry found out about you?"

"He did."

"She was protecting you," I said.

"Yes, she was. I shouldn't have put her in the position. I should have just wondered off into the woods, but it's not as easy to end your life, even when it's not actually life, as you think."

The extra shifts at work weren't for a goat. They were to pay off the librarian. More than one blackmailer in this town.

I went back upstairs and out the door.

Chapter Thirty-Eight

I walked over to Lucy's café, and I sat at the counter. Olive had to wait on me because she was the only one on duty. I told her I wanted to apologize to her before I went out into the woods and possibly never came back. She told me that she didn't accept my apology.

"I just saw your father," I said.

"What? How?"

"I found the secret passage to the basement."

"What was he doing?"

"Just having a bite to eat," I said.

"Now what?" she said.

"Now nothing," I said. "I'm sorry. Sorry for him. Sorry for you."

"Don't you be sorry for me," she snapped

"Sonya Wishbone was murdered, poisoned like the librarian. I'm going to go pick up the murderer. Want to come along?"

She thought about it. "All right. But don't get any ideas. I don't forgive you and we aren't back together."

"I understand," I said.

"I hope you do."

Olive went over to the cash register and told Lucy she had to leave to accompany me to the tower so I wouldn't get killed.

"You sure about this?" Lucy said to me. "You could just wait until she comes back to town."

"I don't think she will," I said. "Not as long as I'm here. I better just pick her up."

"Go on then," Lucy said to Olive. "I need to polish up my waitressing skills, anyway. You never know when I might have to put on the apron again."

We went back into the kitchen. Olive made two sandwiches. She told me to get some bottles from the storage room. She put the sandwiches and chips and empty bottles in her small pack. We filled the bottles with water when we came to the stream. The mountain water was just as cold and fresh as that first day when I wondered into town. We began our walk to the tower. It felt like we were going on a picnic. But once we started walking, that feeling passed. I remembered the way Lord Blackstone had led me on the path, but there were two times when I came to a split I didn't remember.

"The tower is in a different place," I said. "The path has changed."

"Maybe it's better if we don't get there. Maybe Lucy is right. Too dangerous."

"You can go back," I said. "This is really my job."

I don't know what I was thinking. I guess I hoped being together might help my chances of being forgiven. But all I'd done was put Olive in danger.

"You need me," she said. "Lady Blackstone is tricky, even without an attached head."

As we were walking along, a monkey in the trees joined us. Just one monkey.

"Do you know that monkey?" I asked her.

"No," she said.

"Me neither."

"He seems to know you," she said.

"Hopefully not one related to one that was eaten by the lion."

"Care to elaborate?" she said.

"Another time."

The path got steeper, and we were both winded. After a few dozen steps, the grade became more manageable.

"He's very agile," she said. "You have to give him that."

"I think it's a prerequisite for being a monkey. They kick you out if you're not."

The path got very narrow. We had to go single file. I could hear the stream off to the left, but at some point it faded to nothing. Occasionally, the monkey above us would make monkey sounds. Mostly he was quiet, though.

The path widened. We came to a clearing and the tower. We walked up toward the door.

"You ready for this?" I asked.

"Not really," she said.

"Me neither," I said.

Chapter Thirty-Nine

When we were only a few feet away, the huge wood tower door swung open and three obviously dead men walked out. Presumably, Lady Blackstone's cousins. They were the welcoming committee. Clothes still covered in dirt. Their faces were missing chunks here and there. Dead giveaway on their recent digs.

"They were in the Eden Cemetery until not too long ago," I said.

"They aren't like my father," she said.

"Of course not," I said.

"They don't have minds. They're just eating machines. They aren't like him at all."

I got out my sword, and Olive unhooked her Billy club from her belt. The zombies made that zombie noise that they often made in movies and on *The Walking Dead*. One of the writers or the director or some advisor who had brought the zombies to the screen must have encountered real zombies once. They had the grunts down.

That heavy breathing and groaning was very realistic

and primal and I had the urge to run, but I held my ground. I swung the sword and took the head off one. The other two had knocked Olive's club out of her hand and had her pinned to the ground. One was leaning into her face, about to tear it off with its teeth, the jaw opening so wide it could probably swallow a full-grown calf.

She drove a knife into its head, and it fell on top of her. I swung around and with a few steps was close enough to take the head of the other. Olive and I were both out of breath. I sat down next to her.

"I wonder what else she has waiting for us?" Olive said.

"Let's go see," I said.

We went up the stairs and past Lord Blackstone's mother, who wished us a happy day and didn't seem to remember me from yesterday. We were both breathing pretty hard by that point. We had to stop twice before we got up to the roof of the tower where Lady Blackstone was waiting. Her head was resting on a statue of a woman with a beautiful body. Her body was next to the statue, holding a wand.

"Excellent job, Olive. I'd just about decided I'd have to risk poisoning him. This will be better. We'll bury him in the woods. He'll be just another librarian lost to the wilderness."

"You're under arrest for the death of Sonya Wishbone," I said. "She was blackmailing you. I assume that's why you killed her."

"You should have waited in town," she said. "Coming out here was a very bad idea."

"Lucy and Olive told me that but I felt I needed to talk to you face to face. Sonya threatened to tell your husband you'd been sleeping with the librarian. You wouldn't get your head back. She forced you to action."

"Do you know how inconvenient it is to carry a head around?"

I admitted I didn't.

She raised a wand, and I went for my sword. Before I could get it out, Lady Blackstone did some bit of magic that froze my right hand. Olive drew her wand and Lady Blackstone quickly swung hers around and knocked the wand out of her hand.

"Et tu, Olive?"

"You killed Sonya," she said. "You didn't need to. There were other ways."

Lady Blackstone shrugged. "What can I say? I'm evil. Everyone knows that. And now I guess I'll bury both of you in the woods."

While she'd been spending energy stopping Olive and talking, I'd been working on the voice the Amazing Julie had taught me for the hardest hypnotism, possession hypnotism. I found it, and I told the witch to lay down her wand and step back. Then I actually went into her terrible mind for a second to make her drop the wand and step back.

Olive called her wand back to her and had it at Lady Blackstone's throat before she could call her own wand from where she'd dropped it.

"Neat trick," she said to me.

"You pick things up along the way."

"Sure you do," she said.

We made our way down the stairs.

"What's the punishment for murder?" I asked Olive.

"Hanging," she said.

Then she looked at Lady Blackstone carrying her head.

"I suppose we'll have to go a different way for this one."

Chapter Forty

We gave Lady Blackstone to the mayor for safe keeping. He put her in a cell. He had a couple of witch sisters, the Coltrane's, guard her, but she still, somehow, disappeared in the night. Lord Blackstone claimed he would never help her escape. As far as he was concerned, she deserved whatever she got. Diana was quiet about the escape, and I thought she knew more than she was saying, but it was doubtful she had the power to get past the Coltrane sisters.

I knew then I couldn't let it go. I'd known before, but I guess I'd thought maybe I could put it off long enough to avoid the whole confrontation, but I couldn't. I had Marta make the announcement during the morning announcements. At nine o'clock, they started coming in. By 9:05, fifteen of them were in the living room. I'd put out extra chairs for them.

"Is this everyone?" I asked Olive.

"Except for Lady Blackstone," she said.

I waited for them to get settled. When they had, I told them I knew what they'd done.

"You know nothing," one of them said.

"I know you all murdered Barry," I said.

"It was just me," Olive said. "I'm the one who should be held responsible.'

"There you go again," Ms. Wakefield said, "taking all the credit. Not this time. We all had a hand in it. We all wanted to."

The expressions on their faces varied wildly. Defiant, righteous, guilty.

"You all wanted to punish him."

"It had to be done," one woman said.

"We couldn't let him get away with it."

I held up a library book with the Eden Law Code in it. A former judge and several lawyers had put it together a hundred years ago. I didn't think it had been updated since.

"You know about this?"

"I was a lawyer back in my former life," Ms. Wakefield said. "I'll represent all the women if you want to arrest us."

"It was no different from using a date rape drug and then raping us," one woman said, and many others vigorously agreed.

"Magic?" I said.

"Forbidden magic," Ms. Wakefield said. "A man like that thinks he can get away with anything."

"Arrogant little prick," another woman said. "He used a seduction spell on each of us. We never had a chance. Then he stole from some of us."

I held up the book. "Justifiable homicide." I looked at Ms. Wakefield. "The spell he used is forbidden."

"That would be our defense."

We both knew it wasn't an execution crime, according to the book, but maybe it should be. Anyway, no jury in this town was going to convict them. What would be the point of a trial?

"You're free to go," I said.

But I wondered if they would be. Murder, even justified, wasn't as easy to get over as some people thought.

The women hurried out of the library. I was hoping maybe Olive would stay back, but she left with the others.

Chapter Forty-One

I went over to Lucy's for lunch. Olive served me. She was civil, but she made clear with every move of her body that any chance for the two of us to get back to the promising start of a relationship was impossible.

I once met a man on the road who told me that the difference between the possible and the impossible was just two letters. I wasn't giving up.

* * *

Later that day I walked over to the Blackstone's large house and knocked on the door. Lord Blackstone had a manservant named Samuel. He opened the door and gave me a faint, neutral bow.

"Blackstone in?" I said.

"Lord Blackstone is in his study." He laid special emphasis on Lord Blackstone.

Except that he wasn't in his study. He was behind Samuel. He stepped out into the doorway.

"I'll take it from here," he said to Samuel.

"Very good, Sir."

Lord Blackstone's eyes became even blacker when he was angry. "What do you want?" I suppose he didn't like his wife being put in jail, even if he didn't like his wife. Rich people tended to take things personally that made them seem less powerful than they believed they should be.

I'd practiced the calling in the library for hours. I still wasn't sure it would work. I'd only had success with hypnotizing humans. But the ring did give me the ability to call books in the library. I was hoping the boost of hypnosis might help me call them outside the library. I'd memorized some titles, hoping that they would lead the others. I spoke the calling hypnosis. Lord Blackstone tried to shut the door, but I had my leg braced against it. Nothing happened.

At first.

Lord Blackstone started to smile. That was when they came flying out the door. One and then another and then several. Within about twenty seconds, the 42 books were hovering over the Lord's front lawn.

"You can't take those. I paid for them."

"They weren't the librarians to sell."

"I don't care. I paid for them and they are mine."

"These books belong to the town. You're just lucky the amnesty is still on or I'd have to charge you fines."

Lord Blackstone shouted threats as I walked down the street, the books flying behind me in a V formation like geese. It felt like we were all headed home. It was a strange feeling, but not bad, not bad at all.

THE END

. . .

About the author: I did hitch-hike across this country many times in my youth, and worked in a library for nearly a decade. I was adopted, and I do live in a city whose motto is "keep it weird", which are words to live by. I'm not saying I'm strangely qualified to write this story but I am saying I'm strangely qualified to write this story.

Thank you for reading. I am grateful to find readers who seem to have the same kind of twisted (I mean unusual) sense of humor as I do.

If you enjoyed *The Librarian of the Haunted Library* please write a review or leave a rating. They really do help me find an audience for my strange stories. Even a single sentence is great. Thanks so much!

My Book

ALSO, here's a link to book 2. Plenty more in the series after 2.

My Book

ALSO, join my email list if you're so inclined. Get a free book if you sign up. It has horror comedy stories (one that predates this novel and features Kevin) and some stories from other novels in the series that are more mythical in nature. These are all collected in a slim volume for your reading pleasure. If you want to sign up, here's the place to go: https://brianyansky.wordpress.com

Brian

Made in the USA
Columbia, SC
02 November 2024